The Lord's Gambit
An Ormond Yard Victorian MM Romance

Neil S. Plakcy

Copyright 2025 Neil S. Plakcy

This book is a work of fiction. Names, characters, places, and incidents either are products of the author's imagination or are used fictitiously. Any resemblance to actual events or locales or persons, living or dead, is entirely coincidental. All rights reserved, including the right of reproduction in whole or in part in any form.

NO AI TRAINING: Without in any way limiting the author's [and publisher's] exclusive rights under copyright, any use of this publication to "train" generative artificial intelligence (AI) technologies to generate text is expressly prohibited. The author reserves all rights to license uses of this work for generative AI training and development of machine learning language models.

Chapter 1
Chance Encounter
Israel

Israel Kupersmit shivered in the chill March air, his threadbare coat offering little protection against the biting wind. The busy thoroughfare was a parade of London's prosperity: ladies in fitted walking dresses with tiny waists and elaborate bustles, gentlemen in well-cut frock coats and gleaming top hats, even the shop boys in clean collars and sturdy boots.

His own long black coat, once the proper garment of a Jewish scholar, was now shabby and stained. The curled payess at his temples and straggly beard marked him as foreign, other, someone who didn't belong in this world of polished shop windows and elegant tea rooms.

He clutched a stack of flyers in his hands, the gaudy advertisements for one of London's tawdry establishments feeling like lead weights. Through the windows of the tea shop across the street, he saw tables of fine bone china, silver tea services catching the light, plates of delicate cakes that made his empty stomach clench. Well-dressed patrons sat in upholstered chairs, leisurely enjoying their afternoon refreshment without a thought for the cost.

Just months ago, he had been a respected student, welcome in the homes of teachers and rabbis. Now he couldn't even step inside such an establishment without drawing suspicious stares.

"Come to Madame Louise's," he called out weakly, his voice barely carrying over the bustle of the street. He recited the phrase he had been taught, a guttural accent riding beneath the words. "A night of unparalleled pleasure awaits."

Most passersby ignored him, their eyes sliding past as if he were invisible. Others sneered or muttered disapproving comments, drawing their fine wool coats closer as if his poverty might be catching. A group of young clerks in their smart business attire openly laughed at his accent. Israel's cheeks burned with shame, but he pressed on. This degrading task was all that stood between him and complete destitution.

As he extended a flyer to yet another uninterested gentleman, a gust of wind snatched it from his fingers. Israel watched in dismay as it sailed down the street, finally coming to rest at the polished boots of a man unlike any Israel had seen before.

The stranger was tall and lean, with golden hair that caught the weak sunlight. His greatcoat was of fine wool, and even from a distance, Israel could see the crisp white of his shirt collar. Israel took a half-step forward to retrieve the flyer, then faltered, wondering if he should pretend it wasn't his. After all, what gentleman would want to be associated with such advertising? But even as he tried to look away, his eyes were drawn to the graceful way the man bent to pick up the wayward paper, and Israel's breath caught in his throat.

He should run. Surely a gentleman like that would be disgusted by such an advertisement. But his feet seemed rooted to the spot as the stranger approached, flyer in hand.

"I believe you lost this," the man said, his voice rich and cultured. Up close, Israel could see that his eyes were a striking blue-gray, like the sky just before a storm.

"I... yes. Thank you," Israel stammered, reaching for the flyer with trembling fingers. His own voice sounded coarse to him, the accent of his native Poland roughening the edges of the English words.

Their hands brushed as the stranger returned the paper, and Israel felt a jolt of awareness race through him. He had to tilt his head back slightly to meet the man's gaze—the stranger was a good three inches taller—and as Israel reached up for the flyer, he found himself taking an unconscious step closer, drawn into the orbit of this elegant gentleman. But more than that - he saw in the man's storm-cloud eyes a familiar loneliness, a hunger not just for physical comfort but for understanding. Here was someone else who knew what it was to be apart, to live behind careful masks.

"Are you quite all right?" the man asked, his brow furrowing slightly. The genuine concern in his voice nearly undid Israel. How long had it been since anyone had looked at him and truly seen him?

Israel opened his mouth to assure him that yes, of course, he was fine. But the words wouldn't come. He was so tired, so hungry, so ashamed of what he'd been reduced to.

"I..." he began, but his voice cracked as he tried to maintain the careful distance that had protected him these past weeks. But something in the stranger's gentle gaze made the words stick in his throat. "It has been...difficult," he managed finally, his accent thickening with emotion.

"Yes," the stranger said softly. "I know something of difficulty myself." He glanced around the busy street, then back to Israel. The compassion in his eyes was almost too much to bear.

The stranger's gaze flickered over Israel, taking in his worn clothes and gaunt face. But instead of the disgust or pity Israel expected, he saw something else—a flicker of gentle concern in those storm-cloud eyes.

"Perhaps you'd care to join me for a cup of tea? There's a respectable establishment just down the street."

Israel hesitated. Every instinct honed from weeks of hardship told him to refuse—what could this elegant gentleman want with someone like him? And yet... the promised warmth of tea and the unexpected kindness in the stranger's voice made him pause.

"That is... most kind," Israel managed, drawing carefully on his practiced English.

The stranger smiled, and something in that smile made Israel's careful defenses waver, just for a moment.

"I'm Reed Lydney," the man said, offering his hand.

Israel hesitated for just a moment before clasping it. "Israel Kupersmit," he replied.

As they walked toward the tea shop, Israel savored that human touch. It had been so long since he had felt anything like it. A touch that warmed him as much as the man's considerate gaze.

They passed several storefronts that Israel had trained himself not to see—shops whose windows displayed delicacies and comforts far beyond his means. When the stranger stopped in front of an elegant tea shop with gleaming windows and crisp white curtains, Israel nearly continued walking, his habits of self-denial so ingrained that he couldn't imagine entering such a place. But the gentleman reached past him to open the heavy wooden door, and the gesture felt like an invitation into another world entirely.

The tea shop was a haven of coziness and gentility after the harsh London streets. Its walls were papered in a subtle floral pattern and adorned with delicate watercolors of the English countryside. Polished mahogany tables, their surfaces gleaming in the soft light of brass gas lamps, were arranged with precision across the plush carpet. Israel hesitated at the doorway, uncertain if he would be welcome in such a fine establishment, but Mr. Lydney took his elbow and gently propelled him forward.

The air was perfumed with the mingled aromas of bergamot, cinnamon, and freshly baked scones, while the gentle clink of fine bone china and the hushed murmur of polite conversation created a soothing melody. Behind a glass-fronted counter, rows of ornate canisters displayed exotic teas from the far reaches of the Empire, their labels promising flavors from Ceylon, Assam, and Darjeeling.

Israel sank into a plush chair, acutely aware of his shabby appearance. Reed Lydney sat across from him, his posture relaxed yet elegant.

"Two cups of your finest Darjeeling, if you please," Reed told the waiter. "And perhaps some of those delightful-looking scones?"

Israel's stomach growled at the mention of food, and he flushed with embarrassment. Reed pretended not to notice, instead removing his gloves and rubbing his hands together.

"Beastly weather we're having," he commented. "Though I suppose it's positively balmy compared to a Polish winter, eh?"

Israel blinked in surprise. "You know I come from Poland?"

Reed's lips quirked in a small smile. "Your accent. It's very slight, but there's a lilt to your words that reminds me of a Polish chap I worked with for a while. And your name, of course. Israel isn't a common English one."

"You are very observant, Mr. Lydney."

"Reed, please. And observation is a useful skill in my line of work. Or rather, my former line of work."

The waiter returned with their tea and scones, and Israel had to restrain himself from gulping down the hot, fragrant liquid. He took a small, careful sip instead, savoring the warmth that spread through his body.

"The Polish winters, they are ... how you say... brutal? Is correct word?"

"Correct," Reed said.

"I grow up in small village near Warsaw. The snow pile so high sometimes we cannot open front door."

Reed leaned forward, interested. "What was it like, growing up there?"

Israel's eyes took on a faraway look. "Cold, often. And we did not have much. My father say God only give us what we can handle."

"And how did you come to be in London?" Reed asked.

Israel hesitated, then decided there was no harm in telling the truth. "I was no use working for my father, in his cobbler shop. Our rabbi see I study hard, have a talent for numbers. He talk about me, and I am invited to study with a great scholar in London, Rabbi Adler."

Reed's eyebrows rose. "The Chief Rabbi of the British Empire? That's quite impressive."

Israel nodded, a hint of pride creeping into his voice. "I became expert at gematria, a way to use numbers to find hidden meaning in religious texts. Rabbi Adler said I had quick mind for numbers. A kop, we call it."

"A copper? Oh, you mean a head! That's rather clever. And yet here you are, handing out flyers on a cold London street," Reed said softly. There was no judgment in his tone, only curiosity and perhaps a hint of sympathy.

Israel looked down at his teacup, suddenly unable to meet Reed's gaze. "Life take unexpected turns sometimes," he murmured.

Reed reached out as if to touch Israel's hand, then seemed to think better of it. "Indeed it does," he said. "I never expected to find myself living in London either, truth be told."

"Oh?" Israel looked up, grateful for the change of subject. "Where you are from?"

"Derbyshire," Reed said. "My sister Cadence and I grew up on a small estate there. Nothing grand, mind you, but it was home."

"What was that like?" Israel asked, genuinely curious. All he knew of the life of the gentry was what he had read in English novels.

Reed's face softened with nostalgia. "Quiet, mostly. I was always happiest with my nose in a book. Cadence, on the other hand, was forever trying to drag me outside to play."

Israel smiled, picturing a young Reed resisting his sister's attempts to pull him away from his studies. "You were good student then? Like me?"

"Oh yes," Reed chuckled. "I'd hide away in the library for hours, reading everything from Shakespeare to treatises on natural philosophy. Drove my sister mad."

"Sounds wonderful," Israel said wistfully. "To have access to so many books."

Reed's eyes lit up. "Do you enjoy reading as well?"

"Reading, it was... is... great joy for me. But now, not so many chances."

He trailed off, suddenly remembering his current circumstances. The warm cocoon of the tea shop had made him forget, for a moment, the harsh reality waiting outside.

"I know the feeling. When I was in the regiment, books were scarce as hen's teeth." Reed seemed to sense the shift in Israel's mood. "What sort of books do you prefer?" he asked gently.

"I was lucky when I come to England, to board with family of a teacher. He have a large library, and that is how I learned English, when I was not studying with the rabbi. I read novels, mostly, to learn how people live here. And mathematics, of course. But I also have weakness for poetry."

"Really?" Reed leaned forward, his eyes sparkling with interest. "Any particular poets?"

"Keats," Israel said without hesitation. "The teacher had edition of *Endymion* and I memorize much of the book, to dismay of rabbi, who want me to concentrate on Torah."

Reed's smile widened. "Keats is a favorite of mine as well. 'Beauty is truth, truth beauty, – that is all ye know on earth, and all ye need to know.'"

"'Ode on a Grecian Urn,'" Israel breathed, feeling a connection spark between them. For a moment, he forgot about his empty stomach and threadbare clothes. Here was someone who understood the power of words, the beauty of ideas.

They fell into an animated discussion of literature, debating the merits of various poets and sharing favorite passages. Israel found himself gesturing enthusiastically as he spoke, his earlier reticence forgotten.

Reed's quick wit and genuine interest were intoxicating after so long feeling invisible on London's streets. His gaze lingered on Reed's strong hands, the curve of his jaw, the way his eyes crinkled when he smiled.

All too soon, the waiter approached to inform them that the shop would be closing shortly. Israel's face fell as reality came crashing back. He looked down at the crumpled flyers on the seat beside him, then back at Reed.

"I... I go," he said reluctantly. "Thank you for tea, and conversation. It was most kind of you."

Reed reached out, this time allowing his hand to rest briefly on Israel's arm. "The pleasure was mine, truly," he said softly. "Perhaps... perhaps we could meet again sometime? I'd very much like to continue our discussion."

Israel hesitated, torn between hope and pragmatism. "I... am not sure that would be wise," he said finally. "Our worlds very different, Mr. Lydney."

"Reed," he corrected gently. "And perhaps they're not as different as you think."

As they stood to leave, their eyes met once more. For a fleeting moment, something passed between them—a shared appreciation, perhaps, for poetry and conversation. But as they stepped out into the cold London night, reality settled around Israel's shoulders as heavily as his threadbare coat.

Israel clutched his flyers to his chest, steeling himself to return to his dreary task. Carrying it out was all that stood between him and homelessness. Perhaps at some time in the future, he would meet Reed Lydney again, when his circumstances would allow something deeper to develop.

Chapter 2
Bill Collector
Reed

On a Friday morning in early March, the fifth bill-collector to arrive at the house on Bloomsbury Square finally forced Reed Lydney to action. "I beg your pardon, Mr. Lydney," the man said. His name was Raymond, and he was well-fleshed, with red veins in his nose. "But your sister must account for her husband's debts."

"Denis Greenwood—that is, Lord Harlow, is newly in his grave," Reed protested. In handling his father's affairs as the man grew ill, he had some experience of debt collectors. Fortunately, when his father died, followed shortly by his mother, there had been enough money in the accounts to pay all the bills.

They stood in the entry hall of the Greenwood family home in Bloomsbury. The paintings on the wall were all Denis's ancestors, dark-haired and dark-visaged like the late Lord. With Reed's blond hair and fair complexion it was clear to him, if not to Raymond, that he didn't belong there.

But he had to protect his sister. He straightened his shoulders and assumed his full height, several inches taller than Raymond. "And surely the circumstances of his death must grant my sister some time to collect herself and organize her finances."

"These debts have been accruing for long before Lord Harlow's suicide," Raymond said. "The bills from his tailor alone have not been paid for six months."

"Six months!" Reed said.

"And the dues for his club, Lady Harlow's dressmaker, and Harrod's are all at least three months overdue. Your sister must pay these bills or there will be legal action against her."

"Leave them with me, and I will see to them," Reed said.

Raymond nodded. "But I will be back." He turned and walked out the door, allowing a gust of cold air to enter as he did. Reed shivered and walked into the room his brother-in-law had used as an office. The drapes had been left closed, and he opened them, bringing light into the dark room.

Reed could not avoid the chill that came into his voice when he spoke of the Sixth Earl of Harlow. Denis was a brute, and Reed rued the day when his fool of a father allowed the wealthy, newly-named Earl to pursue matrimony with Cadence.

The large walnut desk had belonged to Denis's father, James Greenwood, the Fifth Earl of Harlow, who had died less than a year before. At the time, Reed assumed that in addition to his title, Denis had inherited substantial property along with the family's ancestral home in Gloucestershire.

The light through the tall arched windows was hazy with smoke and fog, so Reed sat at the desk and lit an oil lamp. The desktop was littered with torn envelopes and statements from various vendors.

When Denis Greenwood's father was alive, he had given Denis a generous allowance, which paid for the house in Bloomsbury, Denis's suits and Cadence's ball gowns, and an open table. Reed himself had been a guest there many times.

After Lord James Harlow's death, something had changed in Denis. Reed assumed it was the pressure of his title, but Denis was rarely at home, and when he was, he often rose to anger at the slightest provocation. Cadence, who had always been lively, was lonely, and had leaned on Reed to come stay with her. With the fall of his economic circumstances, he had to agree.

So they had returned to the time of their youth in Derbyshire, before he left home at thirteen to attend the Repton School. He accompanied Cadence to the theater and to salons at the homes of her friends. Though she complained that he was moody and too quiet, he knew she was glad of the company.

Then, two weeks before, Denis had been in a salon at his club, raised a Belgian dueling pistol to the side of his head, and killed himself. Since then, Cadence had barely moved from her bedroom. Reed had coaxed her to eat raisin porridge, the childhood treat they had both loved, but she would consume little else.

He had been relieved not to go out, spending his time reading his way through the impressive library his sister's father-in-law had assembled, waiting for her to rise.

But there was no more time to waste. His heart sank further as he contemplated the piles of unpaid bills, including from the grocer who supplied the food for their meals. This gave him some insight into his brother-in-law's sudden death. He had lost the ability to face his troubles.

Sadly, Reed had little head for figures himself. Though he had graduated from the Repton School with academic success, his focus had been on literature and history, not mathematics. Despite his scholastic aptitude, Reed's plans for university were abruptly derailed when his father fell ill. With the family's properties dwindling and funds needed for Cadence's London season, Reed made the difficult decision to forgo college and enlist in Her Majesty's Army.

The structured life of a soldier suited Reed, and he found himself rising quickly through the ranks. After two years of distinguished service, he caught the eye of his superiors and was offered an unexpected opportunity—a commission as a second lieutenant in Army Intelligence. The promotion was a source of pride, though he had quickly found the term "Army Intelligence" term an oxymoron. Sometimes, at a meeting, he felt there was so little intelligence gathered in a room it was good that they had gas lighting, as many of his fellows were quite dim.

His transfer to the Foreign Office seemed a natural progression, a chance to serve his country in a more cerebral capacity. Yet it was here, amid the quiet halls and close-lipped meetings, that Reed's carefully constructed world began to unravel. An indiscretion, born of loneliness and suppressed desire, led to his abrupt dismissal. The terms of his departure were such that finding new employment became a near-impossible task, his promising career cut short by a single, irreversible mistake.

Now, living under his sister's roof, Reed found himself adrift, his future as uncertain as the fate of the Harlow estate. Denis's generosity had come not at his own expense, but at the expense of all the tradesmen whose bills had been unpaid.

Surely the Harlows had income from somewhere, but he could find little record of that. He stood abruptly and headed to the kitchen, where Mrs. Clarkson held sway. She was only a few years older than Reed and Cadence, but when Cadence needed a cook Mrs. Clarkson, a recent widow, was the only applicant.

"Good day, Mrs. Clarkson," Reed said. "May I have a word?"

Mrs. Clarkson turned to face him. "Of course, Mr. Lydney. How is her ladyship?"

"Still unwell." Reed motioned the cook to the kitchen table and took a seat across from her. "I've come to you on a different matter, however. There is no gentle way to put this, so I will be blunt. Are the grocery bills being paid?"

Her shoulders fell. "Oh, I'm so glad you noticed," she said. "I didn't want to say anything, because of her ladyship's health, but the grocer is becoming more demanding. I've been using up the ingredients in the house but soon we will have nothing to eat if some bills can't be paid."

Reed felt his body sag. "I was afraid to hear that." He remembered a French phrase his mother had often used. "*Pas devant la bonne*," which meant not in front of the maid, or the household staff. He had to keep up appearances.

"I'm working on it," he said. "I'm sure we'll have things sorted quickly."

"Thank you, sir. I don't know if you noticed, but Bess has left us because she couldn't go on without pay."

"Bess was the tweeny? Then who is handling the cleaning?"

"I do what I can. Fortunately Joe is still here, and he helps."

Joe was the boy who lived in the cellar and performed the hard work like bringing in wood and lighting fires.

Reed stood, thanked her, and headed back out into the house. It was time to talk to Cadence.

Chapter 3
Sleeping Rough
Israel

Israel Kupersmit woke shivering, to the sound of children's laughter. He looked around, and the room he was in was just as desolate and barren as it had been when he stumbled into the building the night before. The high ceiling loomed cavernous and forbidding, its tall windows caked with grime that filtered the weak sunlight into ghostly beams.

Dust motes danced in the air, stirred by Israel's movements, while piles of discarded crates and rusted machinery cast ominous shadows across the debris-strewn floor. The damp chill of the Thames seemed to seep through the crumbling brick walls, carrying with it the faint, acrid scent of coal smoke and rotting wood that permeated the forgotten corners of industrial London.

But this old building was not as empty as he had expected. He should have realized something when the door opened so easily. Now, what was he to do?

It had been a long, hard fall from grace. First came his expulsion from the Aldgate Synagogue, when he was shunned by the community that had once welcomed him. The teacher whom he had been lodging with had evicted him shortly after. He'd spent two nights in a cheap hotel until his money ran out, having sold everything he owned except a single set of clothes, his worn coat, and the Star of David hanging from a chain around his neck.

He had wandered the streets of London for nearly a week, sleeping on benches, in doorways, and in a grove of trees in a park. It was hardly sleeping, huddling against the cold winter wind and keeping alert for police or thieves. Then he'd stumbled upon a brothel that catered to men of his ilk.

The brothel occupied a narrow brick house tucked away in a crooked alley off Whitechapel Road, where the grand mercantile avenues of the City gave way to London's shadowy underbelly. The neighborhood was a maze of twisting lanes and dark passages, where gin shops and gaming hells operated behind respectable facades. During the day, horse-drawn carts clattered over the cobblestones, and street vendors called out their wares—hot meat pies, roasted chestnuts, second-hand clothes. As evening fell, a different sort of commerce emerged from the fog-shrouded doorways.

The house itself bore the faded traces of Georgian elegance. Its brick facade had been blackened by decades of coal smoke, and the fanlight above the door was clouded with grime. Inside, what had once been a genteel drawing room now served as a reception area. A massive mahogany bar dominated one wall, its surface scarred by countless glasses and bearing the sticky residue of spilled spirits. Tarnished brass fixtures and grimy mirrors reflected the wan light from gas lamps, casting a sickly glow over the handful of moth-eaten velvet armchairs scattered about.

The air was thick with the cloying scent of cheap perfume, stale tobacco, and the unmistakable musk of human desperation. In one corner, a dusty upright piano stood silent, its ivory keys yellowed with age and disuse, a poignant reminder of more prosperous times.

It was here that Israel found himself that bitter winter evening. The owner of the brothel, a man who dressed in women's clothes and called himself Louise, had looked him up and down, then ordered him to take his clothes off.

"Why?"

"So I can see if you are suitable for employment," Louise said.

The only clothes Israel had were the ones on his back. Shyly, he began to strip, ashamed when his penis began to swell as he did.

"I figured you for a Hebrew from the curls around your ears," Louise said. "Too bad they cut you as a child. Most men who come here don't like that."

Louise examined him, front and back. "This is as big as you get?" he asked, taking Israel's penis in hand.

Israel shivered and nodded.

"You are nothing to my clientele," Louise said. "Too skinny, not well-endowed enough. But I will take pity on you. Can you recognize other men like yourself?"

Israel nodded shyly. He had very little sexual experience, but he was perceptive enough to recognize longing when he saw it.

"Good. I will give you some flyers for this place to hand out. In exchange, I will give you a place by the fire to sleep and one meal a day."

Israel grasped Louise's hand. "Bless you," he said.

"You will bless yourself by convincing men to come in here," Louise said. "If you can't do that, you'll be on your arse again."

The job was harder than Israel expected, especially along the broad sweep of Oxford Street where fashionable shops competed for attention. He would stand near the corner of Berwick Street, where the expensive milliners and drapers gave way to seedier establishments—tobacco shops, public houses, and certain houses whose trade was conducted behind shuttered windows.

Gentlemen hurrying past in their fine wool coats and beaver hats rarely gave him a second glance. Some quickened their pace at the sight of his flyers, while others crossed the street entirely. Those who did look at him were full of pity rather than desire, their eyes sliding away as if ashamed to acknowledge his existence. When fog rolled in from the Thames, as it often did in the late afternoon, the gas lamps cast just enough light to reveal his desperate situation to any passersby.

Louise was unhappy with his progress, counting the few men who actually entered the establishment and finding the numbers wanting. "You're costing me money," became his daily refrain, accompanied by threats to turn Israel back out onto the streets.

After three weeks, Louise stopped him on his way out one morning. The brothel's reception area was a study in faded opulence, its once-rich crimson wallpaper peeling in places to reveal patches of damp plaster beneath.

Louise hadn't shaved and wore a cotton housecoat over his ample frame. "Let me see if you have fattened up," he said.

Israel looked around. The room was empty except for two men in the corner. "Here?" he croaked. "Now?"

"Yes, now." Louise put his hands on his hips, and Israel had no choice but to strip again.

Louise shook his head. "You are still too scrawny." She turned to the two men in the corner. "Come take a look. Would you pay for this?"

The men shuffled over. One was bald as a monk, while the other had straggly brown hair. Upon closer inspection, Israel realized they weren't as old as he expected, no more than forty-five or fifty.

The bald man laughed. "Pay for that? I'd scrape my hands on his hips."

The other man said, "Tell him to turn around."

"Tell him yourself."

The man gestured to Israel. "Now bend over."

Israel was as humiliated as he had ever been as he felt the man's coarse hands on his arse, pulling the cheeks apart. "Too much hair for me," the man said. "I'd scratch my cock to pieces."

"Put your clothes back on," Louise said. He shook his head. "Even my worst customers won't pay for you. Your cock is damaged—no skin to pull or suck on. Your arse is hairy and skinny. And you can't even hand out flyers."

He motioned toward the street. "I've seen you. You stand there like a scared rabbit." He gestured in frustration. "How can you tempt customers when you can barely look at them? I need someone bold, someone who can make promises with just a glance. You're too... proper. Too shy. It's not working. It's time for you to go."

"Go where?" Israel asked.

"Wherever you want. Back to your people, if they'll have you."

"They won't."

"I have done what I can for you. I'm not running a charity here." Louise turned and walked away. And with that, Israel had lost both his job and the corner where he'd been allowed to sleep.

The bald man handed him a shilling. "For the show," he said, and then he and his friend returned to their table in the corner.

Israel pulled his clothes back on and walked outside. The air was frigid, and he tightened his threadbare coat around his neck. Then he walked, without direction.

He had lost track of the days by the time he stumbled on the warehouse. Now, after spending the night on its cold floor—the first time he'd slept indoors since Louise dismissed him—he was awakened by unexpected sounds.

It must be a workday, if there were people in the building. But what kind of job employed children? And why were they laughing?

He had to get out before he was spotted. He didn't want an angry building owner to chase him down the street with epithets, or the police to arrest him. Though that might be best, in the end. At least in jail he would be fed and have a bed to sleep in, or so he thought. He had never known anyone who was arrested.

He stood and crept silently toward the door. With luck, he'd be able to sneak out the back without anyone seeing him.

He opened the door to find a muscular man there. "Who are you and what are you doing here?" the man demanded.

Israel froze, his heart hammering against his ribs. After weeks of avoiding notice—from police, from hostile strangers, from anyone who might bring him harm—he'd walked straight into confrontation.

His fingers gripped the doorframe as he tried to find his voice, knowing his next words might determine whether he found himself in a jail cell, back on the frozen streets, or something much worse.

Chapter 4
Unexpected Guest
Silas

Silas Warner had worked hard all day in the law offices of Richard Pemberton, preparing reports, sitting in on meetings, and even hurrying to fetch a book from the Gray's Inn law library. By the time five o'clock arrived he was bone-weary.

It had been a cold, gray day, with a noxious fog enveloping London, and the evening was no better. Clouds blocked the sky, and the smell of ordure filled Silas's lungs as he sat on the roof of the horse-drawn omnibus, crowded with other passengers.

Even with the noxious smells and the cold wind, Silas was glad that his budget now stretched to cover the penny fare. In the morning, he usually walked from Hackney, where he lived with his lover, the boxer Ezra Curiel. Ezra's generosity, as the owner of the house, allowed Silas to afford small extravagances like omnibus fare and the occasional raisin bun at lunch.

All he wanted was to collapse in the comfortable chair in the living room and relish the smell of whatever Ezra was preparing for dinner. And then a kiss and a cuddle before bed.

Ezra's house was a modest yet well-maintained terraced home, its red brick facade softened by a small front garden where spring bulbs were beginning to push through the soil. The green-painted door opened into a narrow entrance hall, where hooks along one wall held a variety of coats and hats.

A worn but clean rug runner muffled footsteps on the hardwood floor, while a small side table bore a jumble of books on a tarnished silver tray. The scent of furniture polish mingled with the earthy aroma of Ezra's tobacco, creating an atmosphere of comfortable domesticity.

Silas was startled when he stepped into the house. Ahead of him, in the salon, he saw a strange man in his favorite chair. Well, he was not a stranger, exactly, though his appearance was far from the usual. Israel Kupersmit was a religious Jew with a poorly-maintained beard, whom Silas had only ever seen in a shabby long, black coat and a battered fedora.

Kupersmit jumped up. His coat and hat were on the rack by the door, and he wore an ill-fitting jumper that emphasized how skinny he was, and oversized wool slacks tied with a hank of rope in place of a belt.

Silas stood before him, every inch the dandy in his perfectly tailored waistcoat of emerald silk, the intricate folds of his cravat held in place with a pearl pin. His boots gleamed with a mirror polish, and a hint of French cologne hung in the air. Even his dark curls were arranged with artistic precision. It was all thanks to Ezra's money, as Silas had never been able to afford such clothing on his clerk's wages.

"What are you doing here?" Silas challenged.

Ezra came out of the kitchen. His muscled frame filled the doorway, shoulders broad from years of workouts and training. The sleeves of his shirt were rolled up, revealing forearms corded with strength from countless rounds of training.

"Israel is here as my guest," he said. "This morning I found him sleeping in an unused room at the Ragged School. I discovered he has a talent for mathematics, and he was able to engage the children easily."

Silas crossed his arms over his chest. Though he recognized Israel Kupersmit from Ezra's description months ago—the disgraced scholar from the Aldgate synagogue—it still didn't explain why this man was suddenly in their home. Well, it was Ezra's house, and Silas technically an unpaid lodger. But they had made it into a comfortable nest for the two of them.

"When I discovered he has been sleeping rough since he lost his situation with the brothel, I invited him to come and stay with us." Ezra's smile was tight. "That is, if you have no objections."

"You have always been a good and generous man," Silas said, his words slow and deliberate. "It is not my place to object when you have been so kind to me."

He took off his coat and hung it beside Israel's. "Something in the kitchen smells good." He moved in that direction, passing Ezra, who turned and followed him.

"Where is he to sleep?" Silas whispered. "Surely not in our bed?"

Ezra laughed. "Is that what you worry about, my butterfly? No, I will have no man other than you in my bed. Israel can have Rebecca's room."

Rebecca had been Ezra's wife, until his true nature had been revealed, and she had returned to France, where they had both grown up.

"Perhaps you could arrange a bath for Israel before dinner," Ezra said. "I think it has been some time since he bathed. And you could look in my closet for some clean clothes for him. I will arrange to buy him something that fits tomorrow."

"How long do you think he will stay with us?"

Ezra shrugged. "Until he puts some meat on his bones, and finds a way forward in the world."

It was a more open-ended response than Silas wished for, but he would have to settle. He returned to the salon, where Israel sat once again in Silas's favorite chair, his back hunched and his hands on his knees.

"Come, let me show you the bath," Silas said. One of Rebecca's insistences upon moving into the house had been the creation of a small room adjacent to the kitchen with a tub connected to a cold-water faucet. Several large jugs sat on the floor. "Fill one of those and take it to Ezra to heat on the stove, then return here with the hot water. Repeat that process until the tub is full enough for you. You may add cold water from the tap to adjust the temperature."

"It is a marvel," Israel said. "The luxury of a bath in your home!"

"Ezra was very successful in his boxing career," Silas said. "And Rebecca, his former wife, was a good money manager. Come, I will help you."

He filled the first jug from the tap and handed it to Israel, who carried it to the kitchen while Silas filled the next jug. While they waited for the water to heat, Israel asked, "He does not box anymore, Ezra?"

"His manager told him to take a sabbatical after, well, you know." He was sure that Israel knew; half of London certainly did. Ezra had been accused of murder, then vindicated, but his desire for the company of men had been exposed. "His manager hopes that people will forget the trouble, and only remember Ezra's skill in the ring."

They poured hot water into the tub and then repeated the process with two more jugs. "And now he teach at Ragged School?" Israel asked.

Silas nodded. "It is a way for him to maintain his physical condition, and help the children who cannot afford regular schooling." He turned to Israel. "You are a mathematician?"

"Not really. I have some small skill with math, which I used in my study of Torah."

Silas did not know enough about Ezra's religion to understand how mathematics related to the study of ancient texts, so he focused on the tub. When it was full enough, he said, "There is soap on the shelf. I will get you a towel, and some clean clothes."

They kept a stack of towels on the ground floor, so he returned quickly to the bath chamber to see Israel, naked, lowering himself into the water. His ribs protruded from his chest, and his legs were skinny as a chicken's. Silas noted that like Ezra, his cock had been circumcised, as was the custom among their people.

His features spoke of ancient lineage—high cheekbones casting elegant shadows, dark curls with a hint of wave that softened his angular frame. Despite the gauntness of hunger, there was a grace in the way he moved, a certain dignity that transcended physical hardship. His eyes, deep and luminous, held an intensity that seemed to draw light into them—liquid amber flecked with intelligence and a quiet resilience. When he lowered himself into the water, there was a fluid elegance to his movements, like a figure carved from weathered marble, each line telling a story of survival and unexpected beauty.

What if Ezra was attracted to those features, that elegance? Could Israel eventually supplant Silas in his lover's affections?

Silas quickly dropped the towel on the floor and went upstairs to find suitable clothing for their guest. In the end, all Ezra's shirts were too broad in the chest, his pants tailored to his height, which was a few inches below that of Silas and Israel. So the clothes he brought downstairs were from his own closet, a plain white shirt and dark slacks, and a pair of knee-length cotton drawers that he had planned to throw away because they had begun to show wear. Heavy socks to keep Israel's feet warm since his shoes were so run-down.

Israel sat hunched in the tub, the towel around his shoulders, when Silas walked in. "You can stand up," Silas said. "You don't have anything I haven't seen before."

Israel stood, water dripping from his bony shoulders, the towel wrapped around his waist. Silas handed him the pile of clothing. "You may dress for dinner, sir," he said, with mock formality.

When Israel seemed to shrink even further into himself, Silas said gently, "It was a joke. You are welcome to these clothes, and whatever hospitality I can offer you in Ezra's home."

"It is your home, too," Israel said. "Ezra made that very clear to me. That you must approve my staying here."

Silas could not help feeling moved by the poor man's state. "You have my approval, and more. Now, dress, and join us for dinner."

He walked out of the bath chamber. He did not like having his comfortable life upended by this sudden change. Though he and Ezra had often discussed helping others like themselves, the reality of taking in someone from their world, even someone as clearly in need as Israel, made him uneasy. The man's history with the Aldgate synagogue, his fall from grace, his desperate circumstances. All of it hit uncomfortably close to home.

Beyond his fear that Ezra would transfer his attraction to Israel, the poor man reminded Silas of how close each of them was to despair. Silas had lived week to week on his wages; Ezra had been denied his livelihood by gossip and fear. Only those among his acquaintances who were members of the gentry, or had independent incomes, were safe. And indeed he had seen that such safety only went so far. A lord's younger brother, a French diplomat, a graduate of an elite college—all of them could be brought down, Silas and Ezra quicker than most.

He only hoped their compassion wouldn't lead to complications. Not that he truly feared Israel as a rival; despite his handsome face, the man was half-starved and broken by his experiences. But Silas had worked so hard to build this life with Ezra, to create their private sanctuary. Having another man in their home, someone who shared their nature and Ezra's faith, meant letting down the careful walls they'd constructed around themselves.

He swallowed those doubts as he walked to the dining room. Ezra had already set the table. A loaf of challah bread, under a cloth, sat at one end of the table, along with a pair of candles in silver sticks. That reminded Silas that it was Friday night.

"I suppose you receive extra blessings by inviting a stranger to your Shabbos dinner," Silas said.

"The Lord brought you to my side, and that is enough blessing for me," Ezra said. "How is Israel?"

"He is sad and frightened and as thin as a garden rake. Not far from starvation, I should think. Very grateful to you."

"And to you," Ezra said. "I told him this was your home as much as mine."

"And I appreciate that, my dear. Do you need help with anything?"

Ezra had roasted a chicken with spring onions and tiny new potatoes, with a side of young, tender cabbage leaves. Israel's eyes opened wide as he joined them at the table. "I have not seen such a feast in a very long time," he said.

"You will find that Ezra is an excellent cook, as well as a formidable athlete," Silas said, as they sat down.

"You will do us the honors of the blessings?" Ezra asked Israel.

Silas had heard those Hebrew words chanted many Friday nights, but they sounded very different in Israel's voice. Ezra had been raised in France, and for the first time Silas understood that Israel, who had been born in Poland and raised in England, came from a different tradition.

Israel's Hebrew flowed differently—crisp and deliberate, with consonants that seemed to carry the weight of generations. Where Ezra's pronunciation softened and blurred, sliding French-like around the edges of words, Israel's speech retained the sharp-edged precision that Silas had heard in Eastern European Jewish communities.

His vowels held a slightly different music: rounder, more resonant, with undertones of Yiddish that gave each blessing a kind of scholarly gravitas. Silas could hear the difference immediately—Ezra's Hebrew was functional, the result of rote memorization, while Israel's sounded like a carefully preserved manuscript, each syllable intentional and rich with inherited meaning.

"That was lovely, thank you," Ezra said when Israel had finished. He sliced the challah in the glow of the candlelight and Silas poured wine for all three of them.

They talked about the Ragged School, part of an association that taught orphans as well as the children of convicts, drunks, or abusive step-parents. Anyone who could not afford proper clothes for school, or to pay any fees associated. Ezra had stumbled on one of the schools as he was deciding what to do if he could not box. The school had become a passion with him, and Silas was happy to hear that Israel was able to help with mathematics.

Israel insisted on cleaning up, though Silas noticed that his hands shook as he carried plates to the kitchen. Silas and Ezra retired to the salon, where Ezra sat on the divan. Silas was about to take his favorite chair when Ezra patted the place next to him.

"Should I?"

"Israel already knows everything about us," Ezra said.

Silas quirked an eyebrow up. "Surely not everything?"

Ezra laughed. "No, some things remain between us."

"What do you plan to do with him? Get him a teaching job?"

"I don't know. First we must restore him to health and good spirits."

Israel came out to join them then. Already he looked better than when Silas had first encountered him. He was clean and had trimmed his beard, and Silas's hand-me-down clothes fit him better than those he had arrived in.

"Tomorrow I will take you to my outfitter here in Hackney," Ezra said to him.

"But tomorrow is Shabbos," Israel said.

"The shop is run by goyim. As you might imagine, I have difficulty doing business with some members of our community."

"I know that feeling," Israel said. "I very much appreciate your kindness and will do my best not to disappoint you."

Silas watched the interaction between them, struck by how quickly this stranger had become part of their carefully ordered life. Not so long ago, he had called upon every resource he had—his employer, his friends, even his own untested legal skills—to save Ezra from the gallows.

That desperate time had taught him the value of allies, of

reaching beyond their safe isolation when circumstances demanded it. The chapter was still unfolding—Israel's future uncertain, their sanctuary altered, their routine disrupted. Yet seeing Israel in his borrowed clothes, clean and fed, beginning to shed that haunted look, Silas felt something shift in his own perspective. Perhaps their walls needed to be permeable sometimes, if they were to help others as they themselves had once needed help.

Chapter 5
Bankrupt
Reed

Reed stewed over what to do all day Friday after the bill collector left. His lack of a university education was now keenly felt as he struggled to make sense of Denis's financial mess. He finally acknowledged on Saturday morning that he had to let Cadence know her situation.

He knocked on his sister's door, but when she did not answer he pushed the door open. Her bedroom was a sanctuary of feminine refinement, its walls adorned with pale blue silk damask that caught the bleak morning light filtering through lace curtains. The massive four-poster bed dominated the room, its carved mahogany posts supporting a canopy of cream-colored silk that matched the rumpled bedding.

A silver-backed brush and mirror set lay abandoned on the marble-topped dressing table, while discarded mourning gowns draped carelessly over a chaise longue spoke of Cadence's distressed state. The air was heavy with the lingering scent of lavender water and the musty odor of unwashed linens, a stark contrast to the fresh, floral fragrance that once permeated the chamber.

She was still in bed, the quilt and blanket pulled around her. Her blonde curls were matted, her face pale. "I don't want to eat," she said.

Cadence Lydney Greenwood, the Countess of Harlow, was the quintessential English rose. Dainty blonde curls framed a heart-shaped face, her beauty accentuated by all the best powders and creams a lady of 1876 London could find. She was a year younger than her brother, and ever since they were children had been able to twist him to her will.

But now she had to face facts. "I'm not here to force you to eat," he said. "We have bigger problems."

She sat up, clutching her nightgown around her. "My husband is dead. What bigger problem can there be?"

"Denis stopped paying bills at least a month before he died," Reed said. "I've had the fifth debt collector at the door and I finally started to pay attention. I'm afraid you're going to have to do so as well."

"Why would he stop paying bills?"

"Because he didn't have the money. And that's probably why he killed himself."

"That's ridiculous. With his father dead, Denis inherited all his property, along with his title. The Gloucestershire estate alone must generate enough income to support us."

"Do you know if the estate was entailed?" Reed asked. "I realize I should have asked you this already, but I didn't want to disturb you. I'm afraid that time has passed."

"We never discussed it. I know he has a cousin who will inherit the title. But won't the property remain with me?"

"That depends on how it was laid out. If the house in Gloucestershire and the income from the properties belongs to the holder of the title, then it will go to the heir. You don't happen to be with child, do you?"

"What a question to ask!"

"Well, if you were carrying Denis's son, that would simplify matters." He walked over and sat on the side of Cadence's bed. "We have to wake up, dear sister. The bill collectors will not stop coming until they are paid. And we need to know what your situation is."

"I am a widow. The Countess of Harlow."

"You are a widow, that is true. But until we understand Denis's estate, it's not clear what title you retain. You could become the Dowager Countess."

"A dowager! Me! I'm barely twenty-six."

He took her hand. "Please, Cadence, pay attention. I need your help going through Denis's papers."

"I don't know anything about them. Isn't there someone we could hire?"

"With what money!"

Reed was immediately embarrassed by his outburst. But Cadence wouldn't see the truth. They had no money, and perhaps no expectation of any.

Cadence sighed. "Fine. Give me a few minutes to clean myself up and dress. Send Bess up, will you?"

"Bess has left us, because she wasn't being paid. We have Mrs. Clarkson in the kitchen, and Joe to help her. That's it."

"How am I to dress without a maid to help me?"

"Before you had a maid, you dressed yourself. You can do it again. And perhaps you can look at some of your more complicated dresses and see if we can sell them."

She sat up straight. "I am not selling my clothes. Or my jewels."

"We'll see, dear sister. We'll see."

He left her and walked back downstairs to Denis's office. The lamp on Denis's desk was a brass gas fixture, and as he turned it on, its frosted glass shade cast a steady, warm light over the scattered papers. With a gentle hiss, the gas flame flickered slightly, creating shifting shadows among the leather-bound books lining the shelves. The modern convenience of gas lighting, installed during more prosperous times, stood in stark contrast to the current state of disarray in the once-orderly office.

A new worry gnawed at him. If Denis had neglected to pay the gas bill along with the others, they could find themselves plunged into darkness at any moment. The thought of the entire house losing its gas supply sent a chill through him. Without gas, they'd be reduced to candles and oil lamps, unable to cook properly or heat water for bathing. The grand house would become little more than an oversized, ornate cave. He made a mental note to check on the status of the gas bill as soon as possible, all too aware that this modern convenience they'd come to rely on was yet another thread that could unravel in their precarious situation.

He sat at Denis's desk and began to organize the papers there. One pile for unpaid bills. One for unanswered correspondence. Invitations to balls he and Cadence would not attend went in another pile.

Buried deep in the pile he found an envelope from Gloucestershire, and eagerly tore it open. Inside he found two money orders, forwarded by Denis's estate manager. They totaled only ten pounds, but at least they were cash. A note said that other money had been deposited directly into Denis's bank.

He hunted for bank statements. The most recent one showed a balance of only two pounds and ten shillings. But still, every few pounds.

Cadence finally came in. She had put on a pretty blue dress that matched her eyes, and tied her hair up in a scarf of the same color.

"Good news," he said. "I have found some money."

"Excellent! So we can have Bess back?"

He shook his head. "Not even enough to cover the bills. Here, take this pile of mail and help me sort it."

He showed her the piles he'd begun and she began looking through the mail. "An invitation to Lady Smithson's ball last week," she said. "That rotter. He never showed it to me."

"He was dead by then, dear," Reed said. "You wouldn't have been able to attend even if you had known about it."

She sunk down in her chair. "Yes, you're right."

It took another hour, but eventually they had achieved order over the chaos on the desk. The outlook was grim. Cadence owed significantly more in unpaid bills than she had expectation of receiving, at least in the short term. "Someone will have to go to Gloucestershire and speak to the estate manager," Reed said. "To see what we can salvage there."

"If indeed the property belongs to me," Cadence said.

"Did Denis have a will?" Reed asked.

"We talked about it briefly when his father died. But I don't know if he ever had one prepared."

"We should speak with his solicitors," Reed said. "If I recall, he used the firm of Blackwood, Finch & Hartley. Fortunately, I went to Repton with one of their junior solicitors, Antony Wigton. I'll set up a meeting with him."

Reed dashed off a quick note to Wigton along with his calling card, and put it into the mail. When he returned to the office, he found Cadence staring at a round piece of mother-of-pearl. "Is this valuable?" she asked

"It looks like a chip used in whist," he said. "Let me see it."

It had unusual markings, along with the number one. "Probably worth a pound," Reed said. "But we'd have to find out where it came from to cash it in."

He took the chip and put it in the desk drawer. "Maybe it will bring us good luck."

Chapter 6
Butterfly and Bee
Israel

It was a wonder to be clean again, to have a full belly, and to be able to sleep in a bed. Israel should have fallen asleep immediately. But instead he lay there staring at the ceiling.

Rebecca's former bedroom was a modest chamber that spoke more of practicality than luxury. The narrow iron bedstead creaked with each turn, its thin mattress offering little comfort against the chill that seeped through the room's single, drafty window.

Moonlight filtered through the break in the curtains, casting weak shadows across the faded floral wallpaper and illuminating the room's sparse furnishings: a simple pine washstand with a chipped ewer and basin, and a rickety chair draped with Israel's newly acquired clothes. The air held the musty scent of disuse mingled with the lingering aroma of Ezra's tobacco from downstairs, a poignant reminder of Israel's place as an unexpected guest in this humble home.

Israel's mind drifted back to that morning, when Ezra had found him sleeping in an unused room at the Ragged School. He had stumbled into the building the night before, seeking shelter from the bitter wind. The morning's childish laughter had awakened him, and he had been trying to sneak out when Ezra caught him.

Rather than throw him out or call the police, Ezra had listened to his stammered explanation. "You have stumbled into a Ragged School," he said once Israel had finished. "We collect the city's most impoverished children, those who would otherwise roam the streets or work in factories, and give them their first taste of education."

"This is not like any school I have seen," Israel said.

"That is true. We have been loaned the use of this building by the owner who supports our efforts to teach children to read, write, and calculate. Ours are those who no other institution will touch, because they don't have the money to afford proper clothing. Orphans. Street urchins. Children of the poorest laborers."

Israel nodded.

"You appear to be an educated man. What can you teach?" Ezra asked.

Israel shrugged. "Torah. My specialty was gematria."

"Not much need for Torah on the rough streets. And gematria? Isn't that some kind of silly mysticism?"

"Not to those who know it. It's a way to convert the words of the Torah into numbers and then seek hidden meanings in the combinations."

"Numbers," Ezra had said. "You have a head for them?"

"I can add, subtract, multiply and divide," Israel said. "What more is there?"

"Good. The children need someone to help them learn their numbers. If they are to be shop clerks, maids, couriers or apprentices they will need to know how to count, how to tally bills and make change. You can get started with the children in room three."

Israel was startled. Rather than throw him out or call the police, Ezra had was offering him a chance to teach at this very school. Anything to have a roof over his head once more.

"What? Now?"

"No time like the present. Come, I'll introduce you."

He led Israel down the hall and down a set of stairs to a room carved out of a corner of the old warehouse. It had been set up as a classroom and was a stark contrast to the building's industrial past.

Mismatched chairs and battered tables, salvaged from various donations, were arranged in rough rows facing a large slate board propped against the brick wall.

Sunlight struggled through grimy windows, supplemented by flickering gas lamps that cast dancing shadows across the students' eager faces. The air was thick with the mingled scents of chalk dust, unwashed bodies, and the damp mustiness that seemed to seep from the very walls. Despite its humble appearance, the room hummed with the energy of young minds hungry for knowledge, transforming the once-derelict space into a beacon of hope for London's poorest children.

A young woman stood at the front of the room, her face alight with enthusiasm despite her plain, modest dress and the wispy strands of brown hair that had escaped her severe bun. Her slender hands moved in gentle, encouraging gestures as her clear soprano voice led the children in singing a hymn that had been written on the blackboard.

Israel had been startled to read it. "Jesus loves me! This I know, For the Bible tells me so; Little ones to Him belong; They are weak, but He is strong."

This was what the goyim taught their children? He had been raised on a diet of Hebrew prayers and hymns, from the Shma to the blessings over food, wine and candles.

The students were singing along with the young woman. When they came to the end of the chorus, Ezra said, "Thank you, Miss Whitman. Mr. Kupersmit is here now to give a lesson in mathematics."

The students turned and stared at Israel, and he felt how out of place he was, even in such an impoverished setting. His coat, hat, and straggly beard marked him as different, even though he had grown from boy to man in London.

"I'll leave you to it," Ezra said, and he and Miss Whitman left the room.

Israel had never been a teacher, but he had spent enough time in classrooms. "Let's see how many of you know your numbers," he said. Each student had a slate board and a piece of chalk. "Write down as many numbers as you know on your boards."

The children exchanged glances—some wary, some curious. A few shifted uncomfortably, chalk gripped tight in dirty fingers. One small boy with a fresh bruise near his eye stared defiantly, as if daring Israel to mock his ignorance. Another, younger and smaller, clutched his slate like a shield. They had seen teachers come and go, heard promises that meant nothing. But something in Israel's voice—weary but not unkind—made them pause. Slowly, hesitantly, they began to write.

As a dozen young heads bent to the task, Israel was relieved. Maybe he could handle this.

Then he saw the results of the students' work. A mad scramble of numbers in no particular order. Only one boy had managed to put the first five numbers in proper order.

He had a sudden memory of learning numbers himself. Maybe song would help them, as it had him. "Who knows the song 'One, two, buckle my shoe,'" he asked.

A girl raised her hand. "Can you lead us, please?" he asked.

She had a sweet soprano voice. "One, two, buckle my shoe. Three, four, knock at the door. Five six, pick up sticks." Then she stopped. "That's as much as I know."

"A very good start," he said. He picked up a piece of chalk and turned to the board. As the children chanted, he wrote the numbers on the board, then asked them to wipe their slates clean and copy the numbers as he wrote.

He continued to teach the numbers from one to ten, going over them, how to write them and then how to spell them as words. The rest of the morning passed in a blur of teaching, singing, and constant redirection of wandering attention. When Miss Whitman came to the door and announced it was time for luncheon, the children jumped up and scrambled for the door.

Miss Whitman looked at the board. "You have made good

The Lord's Gambit

progress with them. So far I have only been able to get them to write letters."

"It isn't very much," Israel said. "Just a start." Then he hesitated and his stomach grumbled. "Is there luncheon for us as well?"

"Of course. Come with me."

The luncheon at the Ragged School was a modest affair, served on tin plates that had seen better days. A hearty vegetable soup, thick with chunks of potato, carrot, and whatever other vegetables had been donated that week, formed the main course.

Alongside it, each child received a thick slice of brown bread, slightly stale but filling. For those still hungry, there was a large pot of porridge kept warm on a small stove in the corner. The food was ladled out by older students or volunteers, with Miss Whitman overseeing to ensure everyone got a fair share.

The dining area, little more than a cleared space in another part of the warehouse, was filled with the clatter of spoons and the low murmur of hungry children grateful for a warm meal. Israel, too, was grateful; it was the first hot meal he had in more than three weeks.

After the meal he was sent to a different room carved out of the warehouse, with older children. They could all count to twenty but had only the barest understanding of money. He began explaining the most common coins they would have seen, from farthings to shillings.

"How many farthings in a penny?" he asked.

A boy raised his hand. "Four, sir."

"Very good. And how many in a half-penny?"

He picked another boy. "Two, sir."

He continued with the penny, the threepence, the sixpence and the shilling. Then he spotted several piles of stones along one side of the room. He asked the students to gather them up and put them in groups based on their size.

Once they had six piles of similarly shaped stones, he divided them up and paired students for exercises giving change. By the end of the day he was exhausted, but the children were eager to tell Ezra all that they had learned when he stopped by the classroom.

"It looks like Mr. Kupersmit has taught you something useful," he said. "Would you like him to come back on Monday?"

The chorus of yeses warmed Israel's heart. He was equally pleased when Ezra praised him over dinner, in between passing the chicken and slices of the fresh challah.

"They seem very basic skills," Silas had said.

"Of course they are," Ezra said. "These are boys and girls who haven't had the opportunity to study as the three of us have. All they know is what they have learned on the street. And the ability to make change is something they will all need in the future."

The memory of that first day at the Ragged School lingered with Israel as he sat at Ezra's dinner table, the taste of a proper meal still a novelty on his tongue. The clothes Silas had found for him hung loosely on his frame, a reminder of the weeks and months when he had eaten little.

"I see how much the students need to learn," Israel said. "They will need addition and subtraction, and then multiplication and division. How long these children stay with you?"

"It depends," Ezra said. "Some come every day and stay until they have gained the necessary skills for employment. A few months ago, Silas's firm hired one of the boys as a junior clerk."

Israel turned to Silas. "Is true? What skills someone needs for a job like that?"

"It is true, but Luke O'Shea is a special young man. Not only can he read and write and do sums, he has a very quick brain. He still has a great deal to learn, however."

"I could ever get job like that? I have those skills."

He could tell that Silas did not appreciate the question, and wished he could recall it. Sometimes his mouth got ahead of his brain. Other parts of his body, as well. Which had led him to his current predicament.

"Let's focus on bringing you back to health," Ezra said. "And contributing to the Ragged School. If you prove to be a good teacher, I could pay you a few shillings a week."

"Out of your own pocket!" Silas said.

"My dear, we have had this conversation before," Ezra said gently. "I earned this money, so I have the right to decide what to do with it. And be assured, I will never spend more than I can afford. We are secure in this house, and we will always have food on our table."

"But what if you can't return to boxing?" Silas asked. "Surely the money will run out eventually."

Ezra turned to Israel. "Do you know the difference between capital and interest?"

"I think so. Capital is money in bank. Interest is income you receive when that money is lent or invested for you."

"Very good. And what do you know of funds?"

Israel frowned. He had heard men in shul talk about these. "Issued by government or by private companies. They pay interest."

Ezra turned to Silas. "See, our guest understands how one can invest capital in funds and then earn interest on those investments."

"I understand that very well," Silas said. "But what happens when you spend more than your income from those funds? That starts a spiral which can lead to bankruptcy. I have seen that in some of the cases that Antony Wigton handles."

"You must trust me that I keep a very close eye on income and expenses. I will never expose you to such pain."

Israel was fascinated by the back-and-forth between the two men. He had always believed that a relationship such as theirs had to be based in sex. And yet here they were speaking like a married couple about household expenses.

Silas turned to him, and something in his eyes made Ezra shiver. "You cannot continue to dress as you do if you expect to work in a world outside your co-religionists," Silas said.

"It is Israel's choice to dress in accordance with his beliefs," Ezra replied.

Israel felt like a billiard ball caroming between opponents. For a moment, he didn't know what to say. "I retain my belief in God," he finally said. "I see you retain your beliefs, Mr. Curiel, but shave beard and payess. You do not wear a long coat when you go out."

"That is correct," Ezra said. "My father was horrified when I chose to pursue boxing as a profession. Our rabbi considered boxing a violent and un-Jewish activity. My father felt that it conflicted with Jewish values of peace and avoiding unnecessary harm." He sat back in his chair.

"I countered him with arguments of self-defense. Indeed, I first learned these arts when I was growing up in Toulouse and other Jewish boys and I had to endure the taunts and pokes of non-Jews. And then I presented him with the example of Daniel Mendoza, who was a very successful boxer earlier this century. Mendoza was like me, a man of Sephardic Jewish origin."

"I fail to see how that relates to your choice of clothing," Silas said.

"It is all a part of the same thing," Ezra said. "When I understood that I needed to forge my own path, I chose the parts of my religion that mattered to me to carry forward. Things like Shabbos dinner, saying the blessings, and when I can, attending the synagogue. I cut my hair and my beard, and I chose to wear clothing that did not call attention to me."

Silas laughed. "Your tailor would disagree. I know you have your clothes cut to emphasize your musculature." He held up his hand. "Not that I am complaining. Your physique is very attractive to me. I can see why you don't wish to hide it under long coats."

Ezra turned back to Israel. "You will come to understand the relationship between Silas and myself. The way we spar at each other verbally is not an argument, but an expression of our care for each other."

He reached for Silas's hand and squeezed it. Israel nodded. "I will need razor," he said.

Later that night, as Israel lay in bed, he relished the events of the most incredible day of his life. How far he had come from that miserable encounter behind the tavern that had led to his downfall.

He had always thought of his desire for men as a curse, a thing to be hidden away in dark alleys and behind taverns. But seeing Ezra and Silas together showed him something different. They shared a home, took meals together, discussed household finances like any married couple. They had careers and friends who accepted them.

Perhaps there was a way to remain true to his faith while adapting to this new world that had opened before him. A world where men like him could find not just furtive encounters, but real companionship. Real lives.

And now here he was, clean-shaven, with new clothes, with the prospect of honest work ahead of him. As sleep finally began to overtake him, Israel offered up a silent prayer of gratitude. Not the formal Hebrew blessings he had learned as a child, but something simpler and more profound. In Yiddish, he muttered, "Thank you for showing me that there might be a place for me in this world after all."

Lying in Rebecca's old bed as night gathered outside the window, he pondered how much his life had changed in just one day. It was obvious that Silas Warner didn't want him there. But Ezra owned the house, and lived with another man, and Israel knew he had to understand he was only to be a lodger, nothing more.

That reminded him of something Ezra had said at dinner. "At the end of the day, I am the bee and my lover is the butterfly, and we coexist together in our own garden."

Israel smiled in the darkness. Perhaps he too would find his own garden someday. For now, he was grateful just to have shelter, and perhaps a chance to be useful again.

Chapter 7
Never a Saint
Reed

Reed slept poorly on Saturday night, and spent much of Sunday morning in bed, feeling thoroughly miserable. Somehow, he had failed to protect Cadence, as he had promised both their parents on their deathbeds.

His bedroom was modestly appointed, befitting a guest chamber in the home of a peer of the realm. A sturdy oak wardrobe stood against one wall, its doors slightly ajar to reveal Reed's suits, dinner jackets and trousers. A small watercolor landscape of his and Cadence's childhood home in Derbyshire was propped against the mirror on the dresser.

The usually crisp linen sheets were tousled on the brass bed beneath a faded quilt. A prized photographic portrait of his parents was displayed in a simple frame on the bedside table, beside a gold pocket watch inherited from his father.

Two books rested there as well. One was a volume of military history, the second a copy of *Endymion* by John Keats. His brief connection with the poor man handing out fliers had caused him to find that in the late lord's library, and when he had brief moments he dipped into it.

As he sat back against the headboard, he reflected that it wasn't his fault that Cadence had married Denis, nor that he had turned out to be a rotter. Nor was his brother-in-law's suicide on his conscience. But he should have stepped up immediately after Denis's death, sorted through the bills and taken over responsibility for the household, especially as Cadence was in mourning.

He had trouble understanding how deeply she felt. Every morning, he thought she'd wake up, cheered by the fact that her moody, difficult husband was gone. And yet she seemed to miss him greatly. Reed's past experiences, from Repton to the army, had ill-prepared him for the depth of feeling Cadence seemed to have for Denis.

Denis and Cadence spent very little time together, and when he was around he was often angry about small things. Cadence covered for him and Reed hadn't been able to tell if she loved Denis, or was simply playing her cards close to her chest.

Then he died, and Cadence plunged into mourning. If it hadn't been for the pesky bill collector, they might still be in the same situation, living together and avoiding any talk of the future.

Eventually, late in the afternoon, he dressed and went out.

The March sky was gray, the wind blustery, and he huddled into his overcoat as he walked. He thought of Israel Kupersmit, and the brothel he had been advertising, but he had no money to pay for companionship. He knew of a pub where he might connect with other men, but he didn't feel like talking. Without thinking he ended up at the edge of Hyde Park.

His cock swelled as he considered heading into the park. Maybe a quick encounter was what he needed to relieve some tension. Get some good feelings going that would carry over to Monday morning when reality would set in once again.

He walked down Bayswater Road to an entrance to the park that ran between two small woods. He had almost come to the Carriage Road when he heard angry shouting. "I wasn't doing nuffink!"

Soon a bobby came into view, dragging a young man in a coarse coat. His trousers flapped open. "Sure you weren't," the bobby said. "Tell that to the judge."

Reed stepped into the shelter of a tree until they had passed. He was shaking and it took him a moment to compose himself. That could have been him. Caught in flagrante with another man's mouth on his cock, as he had been in the past. And without the backing of the Foreign Office, this time he might have ended up in gaol. Whatever tatters of a life he still had, ruined.

He waited until the bobby and the unfortunate man were out of sight, then hurried back to Bayswater Road, and from there to Bloomsbury Square. By the time he reached the shelter of home he was cold and exhausted, berating himself over and over for being a fool.

He did not sleep well, but he was pleased when Cadence joined him for breakfast Monday morning, though she only picked at her oatmeal. She wore her dressing gown and had not pinned up her curls, and he was reminded of nursery breakfasts together before he left for Repton.

While they were eating, Joe, the boy, brought him a response from Antony Wigton by messenger.

"Excellent!" Reed said, after he read the note. He looked up at Joe. "Is the messenger still here?"

Joe nodded. "Yes, he said he would wait for a response."

Reed stood and found a calling card on the side table. He scrawled, "Eleven o'clock it is. See you then," with his initials. He handed it to Joe, who returned to the front door.

Reed sat back down at the table and addressed his sister. "Wigton is happy to meet with us at the offices of Blackwood, Finch & Hartley at 12 Lincoln's Inn Fields at eleven o'clock this morning."

"Must I go with you?"

"I'm afraid you must. You are the widow and the debtor; I am but your brother and advisor. If there are papers required they must have your signature."

"You will have to send Mrs. Clarkson to help me dress then."

"Mrs. Clarkson will be busy in the kitchen. I can certainly lace up the back of your dress if necessary. I did it enough times when we were young."

Cadence frowned. "I dislike not having a maid. It took quite some time to train Bess appropriately so that she could be both a tweeny and a ladies' maid."

"Well, you will have to face facts. You are perilously close to bankruptcy. You may no longer be able to afford Drayton House, or even this home where we live. I have very little ready cash myself, and though I invested what I inherited after mother's death, the interest is not enough to support me. I will get a job as soon as we have settled things, and then I may be able to help you."

Cadence looked like a child who had lost a favorite toy. The edges of her mouth drooped and tears pooled in her eyes.

"I do not mean to hurt you, dear sister," Reed said. "But we must face facts if we are to survive. Antony Wigton was a good chap at Repton. His father was a prosperous landowner in Derbyshire, and I was his family's guest several times at their home. I hope he will treat us well."

"And he is now a solicitor?"

Reed nodded. "He read law for seven years at the Inns of Court. And after two years of further study, he joined Blackwood, Finch & Hartley. I have not seen him in some time, but the fact that he responded to my note so quickly is a good sign."

He smiled slightly, remembering. "At Repton, Wigton and I were both in Mr. Drummond's Greek class. We spent countless hours together translating Homer, debating the true meaning of honor and duty. Wigton always argued that loyalty to friends outweighed all other obligations."

Unless his troubles had made him a curiosity Wigton was ready to shun in person. Perhaps those youthful debates about honor meant nothing in the face of adult realities.

Chapter 8
Suspicion
Israel

Monday morning, Israel woke early, his stomach churning with anxiety about the day ahead. He dressed carefully in his new clothes, still marveling at how different he looked without his beard and payess. As he adjusted his collar in the mirror, he caught sight of Ezra watching him from the doorway.

"Ready for another day of molding young minds?" Ezra asked with a smile.

Israel shrugged. "I am not sure I am meant to be a teacher, Ezra. Friday was... challenging."

"Come, walk with me to the school," Ezra said. "We can talk on the way."

As they walked through the bustling streets of London, Ezra offered words of encouragement. "Teaching takes practice, Israel. You have knowledge to share, you just need to find the right way to convey it."

Israel nodded, but his doubts lingered as they approached the Ragged School.

"Do you know what you will teach today?"

"It took me time to learn numbers," Israel said. "Much repetition needed. So today I go back to what they study on Friday. Order of numbers for young ones, money for older."

Ezra nodded. "Good. I know they won't be like the students at your yeshiva."

"Yes, Rabbi Adler is strict teacher. Boys must be quiet and do their work. No girls, no play. Your school very different."

That morning it was hard to get the boys and girls to focus on math. He asked them to repeat what they had learned on Friday, but little had remained in their brains over the weekend. Almost all were able to write the numbers from one to ten on their slates, but most did not understand the proper order.

The youngest ones were easily distracted. "Why do you look different today from Friday?" one boy asked.

"You look cleaner," a girl said. "Did you take a bath? My mam makes us bathe every Saturday. Does your mam do the same for you?"

Israel smiled, touched by the children's directness. "My friends helped me clean up," he said simply. The truth was more complicated —Ezra's kindness, the unexpected bath, the clean clothes that still felt strange against his skin—but these were children who did not need to know the full weight of his recent past. "Cleanliness is important," he added, remembering his own mother's teachings. "It shows respect for yourself and for others."

He paired them up once more, asking them to count the numbers on their partner's fingers. But that led to several instances of students playing a game with each other called pat-a-cake, which he had never heard of. And that led to wrestling and hair-pulling, which he had to stop.

As the morning wore on, Israel found himself constantly redirecting wandering attention and breaking up small squabbles. By lunchtime, he was once again exhausted.

He ate his lunch with Miss Whitman, whose Christian name, he learned, was Sarah. She was a Quaker and came to teach every day while waiting for her fiancé to put together enough money so they could marry.

"How do you keep them in order?" he asked.

She smiled sympathetically. "It takes time to develop a rapport with the children. They'll settle once they get to know you better. And we sing a lot. Mostly hymns but occasionally children's songs. I find that making them sound out the words helps with their reading."

"Hard to do that with mathematics," he said.

Suddenly she began to sing. "Five currant buns in the baker's shop, Round and fat with a cherry on the top. Along came Polly with a penny one day, bought a currant bun and took it away. Four currant buns in the baker's shop, round and fat with a cherry on the top. Along came Ted with a penny one day, bought a currant bun and took it away."

She looked at him. "Surely you know that."

He shook his head. "When we sang at school it was only in Hebrew."

She wrote out the rhyme for him. "I know it's only counting to five, but it's a start," she said.

If anything, teaching the older boys and girls was even worse. They understood the importance of knowing money, and making change, but that was it. They weren't interested in any higher functions, and he couldn't get them to focus on their times tables.

"Do birds count?" a boy asked. "How do they know how many seeds to eat?"

And on, and on, for hours. Every time he tried to lead them back to their numbers, someone had a new distraction.

The afternoon brought a small victory when Israel managed to engage them in another game of making change with pebbles. For a brief moment, he felt a glimmer of satisfaction as he watched them work out the sums.

Toward the end of the day, Ezra appeared at the classroom door. "How are you all?" he asked, and then chorused back that they were fine or well.

He demonstrated a simple exercise, his movements fluid despite his bulk. The children watched in awe as he lifted one boy effortlessly overhead, his muscles rippling beneath his shirt.

After they left, he turned to Israel. "How did it go today?" he asked.

Israel sighed. "Better in some ways, worse in others. I am not sure I make any progress."

They walked home together, with Israel recounting the day's events in detail. Ezra listened patiently, offering advice where he could.

"You will improve with time," Ezra reassured him. His powerful hands, calloused from punching bags and skipping rope, gestured as he spoke. Even in repose, his body held the coiled energy of a fighter.

"Maybe tomorrow I will teach with you. We can combine gymnastics with counting. I've found that when you wear out their bodies their minds have a chance to function."

Israel shook his head. "Maybe I am not to be teacher."

"You're being too hard on yourself," Ezra said as they reached the house. "Remember, many of these children have never had any formal education before. Every little bit helps."

They had an hour before Silas would return home, and while Ezra prepared dinner he set Israel to looking through Silas's books for anything that might help him in teaching.

He pulled down a volume on basic accounting and began to leaf through it, making notes on a scrap of paper. When Silas returned home and found Israel among his books again, his face tightened with annoyance.

"What are you doing!" Silas demanded. "Those are my books."

Ezra came out of the kitchen. "I suggested he look through them for inspiration in his teaching," he said. "You don't mind, do you?"

Silas looked from Ezra to Israel and then back. "As long as you're careful," he grumbled.

As Silas nodded and turned away, Israel couldn't help but notice the clerk's lingering look of suspicion. He knew he was an outsider here, in Ezra and Silas's home and in this world of work so different from his religious studies. But he was determined to prove himself, one way or another.

Chapter 9
Old School Chum
Reed

After their breakfast conversation, Cadence went upstairs to dress. Reed considered what he needed to wear as well, but before meeting with Antony Wigton, he had to visit Denis's bank.

He summoned Joe to polish his leather boots, then donned a good white linen shirt over riding breeches. He stood before the cheval mirror and tied a white silk cravat, and by the time he had it done perfectly Joe returned with the boots and helped him pull them on.

Then Joe brought his greatcoat and top hat. It was important that he not give off any aura of financial need when he walked into the bank.

He stepped out into the bustling London street and adjusted the collar of his coat. The clop of horses' hooves on cobblestones and the rattle of carriage wheels provided a familiar backdrop to the bustle of morning commerce. As he walked, Reed sidestepped puddles left by the night's rain and nodded politely to ladies sheltered beneath lace-trimmed parasols.

The bank's imposing facade loomed before him, its Grecian columns and ornate stonework a testament to the power of commerce in Victorian London. Inside, the high-ceilinged lobby buzzed with activity, the murmur of voices mixing with the scratch of pens and the clink of coins. Gas lamps cast a warm glow over the polished mahogany counters where clerks attended to customers with brisk efficiency.

Reed approached the assistant manager, a portly gentleman with mutton-chop whiskers, who had assisted him after Denis's death. The man's eyes widened in recognition, and he ushered Reed to a private alcove, away from the curious ears of other patrons.

Reed settled into the plush leather chair across from the assistant manager's desk, the weight of his responsibility pressing upon him. The portly gentleman leaned forward, his gold watch chain glinting in the lamplight.

"Mr. Lydney, it's been some time. I trust all is well with the Countess?" The manager's tone was solicitous, but Reed detected a hint of curiosity beneath the polite inquiry.

"As well as can be expected, Mr. Hawkins," Reed replied, forcing a wan smile. "We're in the process of sorting through Lord Harlow's affairs."

Hawkins nodded, his eyes flickering to the money orders Reed had placed on the desk. "I see. And these are…?"

"Income from the Gloucestershire estate," Reed explained, keeping his voice steady despite the knot in his stomach. "We're working to ensure all accounts are in order."

The manager's bushy eyebrows rose slightly. "Very prudent, Mr. Lydney. Very prudent indeed. There have been… whispers, you understand. Nothing concrete, of course, but in banking circles…"

Reed straightened in his chair, his jaw tightening. "I can assure you, Mr. Hawkins, that we are taking every measure to address any concerns. The Countess's affairs will be managed with the utmost propriety."

Hawkins seemed to consider this for a moment before nodding. "Of course, of course. We at the bank are always here to assist in any way we can. Perhaps a meeting with our financial advisors might be beneficial?"

"Thank you, but that won't be necessary at present," Reed said, his tone brooking no argument. "If you could simply process these money orders, we would be most grateful."

As Hawkins busied himself with the transaction, Reed exhaled slowly, acutely aware of the precarious nature of their situation. He only hoped his show of confidence would be enough to keep the wolves at bay, at least for now.

When he left the bank, he had cash in hand and was more reassured. He visited the grocers, where he paid off Denis's debt and ensured that there would be food in the house on Bloomsbury Square.

He had enough left over to pay Mrs. Clarkson and Joe what they were owed, and leave some coins in his pocket. By the time he returned to Bloomsbury Square, Cadence had finished her bath, and he helped pin up her curls and tighten her corset.

"It is a great shame you do not have an affinity for women," Cadence said. "You would make a great husband."

It was the first time she had directly addressed the problem that had caused him to lose his job with the Foreign Office.

"Could you ever force yourself, do you think, if a suitable woman were to appear?" she asked. "One with money?"

"That would hardly be fair to her," Reed said. And after a moment he added, "Or to me. No, I expect I will have to make my way in the world on my own. Perhaps now that time has passed, the scandal of my firing will have dissipated and I may be able to find a job that would pay my way."

He donned his greatcoat and hat once again, and sent Joe out to hail a carriage to take them to Lincoln's Inn Fields. It wasn't far along Southampton Row and Chancery Lane, and he would have preferred to walk if he was alone. But he could not expect Cadence to make such a journey on foot.

Signs of spring were all around, from the buds on the horse chestnut trees to the crocuses and snowdrops blooming in Russell

Square. Swallows swooped and dove over the street as the carriage rocked over the cobblestones.

Wigton's firm was in a Georgian townhouse converted for professional use, which was dignified but not overly ostentatious. As he helped Cadence out of the carriage, he stopped short. Suppose Wigton had heard of the reason for his dismissal from the Army? What if he had only called them here to gloat at their troubles?

He steeled himself. So what if Wigton knew? Reed was bringing him business. And if Wigton didn't want the work, there were other solicitors who would.

He opened the front door for Cadence, to find a small, formal space with clerk at a desk. He introduced them, and the clerk hurried up a curved staircase with carved wooden banisters.

Reed took that moment to look around. Dark wood paneling, a thick carpet, and a gas lamp on the clerk's desk, which had several neat piles of files on it.

A few moments later the clerk descended, followed by Antony Wigton. He looked much the same as he had the last time they'd run into each other, when Reed was still employed at the Foreign Office. His blond hair, a few shades darker than either Reed's or Cadence's, was slicked down and he wore a well-fitted navy suit with a red tie. The way Reed himself might have dressed if he was still employed.

"This is an unexpected pleasure," Wigton said, reaching out to shake his hand. "How are you, Lydney?"

"Not good, I'm afraid," Reed said. "May I present my sister, the Countess of Harlow?"

Wigton took her outstretched hand in his. "A pleasure, I'm sure. Though you have my condolences on the loss of your husband."

"Lord Harlow's death is what we need to talk to you about," Reed said.

Wigton turned back to Reed. "Well, let's get onto it. Our clerks have offices on this floor, though we are short-staffed at the moment. My office is on the second floor along with our library and meeting

The Lord's Gambit

rooms. The partners are all up in the heavens above us. That is, the third floor," he added with a smile.

They followed him upstairs. "I'm afraid my office is a bit small," he said. "Come into the meeting room with me." It was well-appointed, with a large polished oak table, comfortable chairs, and bookshelves lining the walls. Four-over-four windows looked out to a tree in bud.

The furniture was heavy and ornate, much like that at Cadence's home in Bloomsbury, and Reed saw her relaxing. A portrait of one of the founding fathers of the firm hung on the wall. The shelves were lined with law books and case files.

"I've ordered tea," Wigton said, as he sat across from them. "Now, what can I do to help?"

Reed looked at Cadence, who appeared happy to let him take the lead. Reed briefly sketched out the situation.

"We can certainly research the title and how it passes, and help you organize Lady Harlow's debts and income," Wigton said. "We're a bit short-staffed right now. We need to hire another clerk and a bookkeeper as well before we could handle your sister's case."

"It's rather urgent," Reed said. He opened the leather folder he had brought with him and showed Wigton the debt-collector's demands, as well as the sheaf of unpaid bills he found in Denis's desk.

Wigton took the paperwork and flipped through it. "Yes, your brother-in-law left things in a bad state. Is there income?"

"I'm not sure. It seems Lord Harlow sold off a great deal of the income-producing properties."

"Was he a gambler?"

Reed nodded. "But I never realized he had let things go so badly."

Wigton blew out a breath. "I won't sugar coat this, Lydney, and milady. Things don't look good. But give me a day or so to see what I can organize. No promises, yet, but for an old school chum I'll give it my best shot."

Wigton had a boy summon a carriage for Reed and Cadence.

"You'll see. Things will work out," he said as he walked outside with them. He clasped Cadence's gloved hand in his own and smiled at her. "I will do my best work for you."

In the carriage, Reed teased his sister. "You are still turning heads, my dear," he said.

"Oh, pshaw," she said, but she smiled, perhaps for the first time since Denis's death.

Chapter 10
Money Troubles
Silas

Silas was surprised to find Richard Pemberton already in the office at Gray's Inn when he arrived on Monday morning. The barrister had lit an oil lamp and sat in his office, looking through account books. "I'm sorry, sir," he said. "Did we have an early meeting?"

Pemberton shook his head. Well into his forties, Pemberton was a commanding figure, though heavier than he should have been. A few gray hairs nestled amongst the black. "No, I could not sleep, worrying about finances, so I came in early to see."

"I have all our invoices out to be paid," Silas said. He took his coat and hat off and hung them on pegs in the outer office, then joined Pemberton.

"Yes, you've done well with that. But we are short on new cases and I am concerned that I can continue to pay you and Robb and young Luke."

Silas sunk into his chair. He had seen this coming, but hadn't had the nerve to mention it to Pemberton. And what could he as a clerk do? He couldn't find cases for Pemberton to prosecute, though he had done that once with Ezra's murder charge.

"You have some meetings scheduled later in the week," Silas said. "They may result in new clients."

"Yes, I hope they will. But don't you fret, lad. Our business rises and falls with the crime rate and the nefarious doings of those in power. We will manage."

Silas returned to his desk and began going through his work. His job was to manage Pemberton's calendar, suggest rates for clients, and handle any kind of research necessary. Luke O'Shea was his junior clerk, sent to check out records and fetch library books, while Robb was the errand boy who delivered messages and bills.

The three of them were busy all morning, though Silas occasionally paused to worry about what might happen if Pemberton had to cut back. Luke was a smart young man, but he needed much more seasoning and experience. He and Robb would struggle to find new employment.

At one o'clock, Antony Wigton arrived without an appointment. "Is himself available?" he asked Silas.

Because of their financial deficit, and the chance that Wigton had a new client he needed represented in court, Silas would have interrupted his boss even if they were busy. He rose and knocked on Pemberton's door. "Mr. Wigton is here, if you can meet with him."

"Certainly, send him in. And come along with him, with your note pad."

Silas ushered Wigton into Pemberton's office then took a chair at the side of the room. "An old school chum approached me this morning with a case," Wigton said, and Silas heaved a sigh of relief he hoped was not noticed by either man.

"Not something for you to prosecute, however, I thought I might be able to utilize some of your resources."

Well, that wasn't as good. But what kind of resources?

"What would you need?" Pemberton asked.

"Have you heard of two solicitors who set up their own firm called Fairfax and Longbottom?" When Pemberton nodded, Wigton continued. "They have poached two members of our staff in the last two weeks. The clerk I usually work with, and our firm's bookkeeper. We haven't had the time to hire permanent replacements. In order to handle this new case, I need temporary help."

"My staff happen to have some time at the moment," Pemberton said. "Tell me about the case."

Wigton began with the issue of entailment. "The first thing we need to discover is the conditions of Lord Harlow's title. He and the Countess were only married for a short time, and as far as we know there is no legitimate issue. Which means, according to the Countess's brother-in-law, that the title passes to a distant cousin."

"And you need to know who inherits the property," Pemberton said. "I assume there is no will?"

"Not that we have found. Denis Greenwood was a young man in good health when he assumed his father's title, and when he died. We need to contact the firm of solicitors who handled Lord James Harlow's estate to see what they know. Since they are in Gloucestershire I thought we could begin with the Court of Chancery and then Somerset House about wills and probate records."

"Silas is well-informed on searches in both locations," Pemberton said. "I can make him available to you."

"Excellent. And then we have the matter of organizing the late Duke's debts and assets." He turned to Silas. "How good are your mathematical skills?"

"They are average, sir," Silas said.

"Silas handles all the billing for the firm quite well," Pemberton said.

"This is a big task," Wigton said. He opened a leather folder and withdrew a sheaf of bills, which he handed to Silas.

It was darker in his corner, so he moved his chair closer to Pemberton's desk, and the light. "Oh, my. These are complicated," he said after a moment. "Some small amounts have been paid toward these accounts, but there are balances and interest to be counted. I would need to focus all my time on this, for at least a week or two."

Wigton frowned. "When there are other things you need to work on." He turned to Pemberton. "Have you no other resources?"

The barrister shook his head. "My junior clerk is very raw and I would not trust him with matters of such complexity. You need someone with a real mathematical head."

Suddenly Silas had an insight. Ezra had raved over Israel Kupersmit's math skills. Could he handle something like this?

He had seen the way the young man had been cleaned up. But there was still the matter of his religion, which some might object to. "Would it matter if the person was of the Hebrew faith?" he asked.

"Not at all," Wigton said. "Those people are known to be very good with numbers."

"Did you have someone in mind?" Pemberton asked.

"A young man whom Ezra has begun to mentor as a teacher at his Ragged School," Silas said. Wigton had been Ezra's solicitor so he was quite familiar with the ex-boxer. "According to Ezra, his religious studies included a great deal of mathematical calculation, and he is doing a good job teaching."

"Could we hire him for a short time?" Pemberton asked. He turned to Wigton. "With your permission, and at your client's cost?"

"We need to move carefully," Wigton said. "The state of the Countess's finances is very unclear. If the estate is entailed, then all she has is debts..."

"Then she can't pay either of us," Pemberton said. He looked at Silas. "Well, shall we roll the dice?"

Silas admitted his own selfish motives. While he didn't want to work with Israel, he did want the man to become self-sufficient enough to move out of the house in Hackney. This might be his ticket. If he did a good job, perhaps Wigton's firm would hire him permanently.

"I think it's worth a shot," Silas said. "But first I must go to Somerset House and determine the conditions of the estate. With a few hours of my time, we will know if there is money available to mount a full investigation."

"Excellent," Pemberton said. "Silas, draw up the appropriate contract between ourselves and Blackwood, Finch & Hartley. How soon can you get to Somerset House?"

"I have some matters to finish up before the end of the day. I can begin at Somerset House tomorrow." And if Israel was amenable, he'd take the ragged man with him.

Silas rode the omnibus home on Monday evening, thinking about how best to take advantage of the opportunity Antony Wigton had presented that morning, if indeed there was money in the estate to pay them. Otherwise, Wigton's client might end up in debtor's prison, and Pemberton's perilous financial condition would continue.

When Silas walked into the house, Ezra was in the kitchen, where something was sizzling on the hob, and Israel was on the floor with several books around him, and a scrap of paper he was using to take notes.

Silas hung his coat and hat. He was at first annoyed that Israel was looking at his books, but he reined in his irritation. "Do you like teaching?" he asked Israel.

Israel looked up from the floor. He carefully closed the book he had been reviewing and stood up. "No, I don't. Ragged School very different from yeshiva. I am very good at writing out sums and totaling them. But I do not know enough of what these children need to learn."

"Well, I may have another opportunity for you," Silas said. "We'll talk after dinner."

Ezra came into the dining room carrying a big pot of stew. Strands of beef floated in a heavy broth with chunks of potato and carrot. There was a loaf of crusty bread to mop up the liquid with, and they all fell to eating.

It was not until after they had finished eating that Israel asked, "What kind of opportunity you mean?"

"What do you know of solicitors and barristers?" Silas asked.

"Very little."

Silas gave a quick lecture on the role of the two parties of the legal system. "A solicitor came to us for help this afternoon in researching the estate of a recent suicide," he continued. "I am well acquainted with such research, but the skills of a bookkeeper are also necessary in this case, and neither of our firms have such a person on staff at the moment."

"My uncle is bookkeeper," Israel said. "I often helped him balance his accounts for clients. I know a little of assets and liabilities and so on."

"Excellent. Maybe you can fill this need for Barrister Pemberton. Can you come to the office with me tomorrow morning?"

Israel looked at Ezra.

"Of course, go," Ezra said. "I'm sure Miss Whitman will have a few songs for the children to keep them busy. And someone else will come along to handle the mathematics if necessary."

Chapter 11
Summons
Reed

When Reed and Cadence arrived at Bloomsbury Square after the meeting with Wigton, Joe greeted them eagerly at the front door. "A message for Mr. Lydney," he said importantly, and handed it to Reed.

"Not another debt collector, I hope," Cadence said.

Reed immediately recognized the letterhead of the Foreign Office, and he shivered with fear. Was he being called to account for something?

The message was short. "Lydney. Please come to my office tomorrow morning at 10 to discuss a matter of utmost importance. Yrs, Gervase Quinn."

Cadence put her hand on his arm. "You have gone all white, brother. What is the matter?"

He showed the note to his sister. "Any idea what this is about?" she asked.

He shook his head. "But it can't be good."

"Well, the tone is pleasant enough, if a bit peremptory. He uses please and closes with yours."

"That is the language of diplomacy," Reed said. "Something

Gervase Quinn is fluent in. It doesn't mean the matter is a positive one."

"You stood by my side as you forced me to confront the mess Denis left for me," Cadence said. "Whatever awaits you tomorrow, I will be here for you." She leaned up and kissed his cheek lightly. "And now I must get out of this corset! I had forgotten how uncomfortable these things are."

How much was one man meant to endure, he thought, as he pulled off his coat and hat and walked into the salon. The room, with its richly patterned William Morris wallpaper and heavy velvet drapes, seemed to mock him with its air of faded opulence; the ornate gilt-framed mirrors reflected a man he barely recognized, worn down by circumstance and worry. First the ignominy of his arrest, and the loss of his job. Then Denis's death.

True, he hadn't cared much for the man, but at least his brother-in-law had put a roof over his head and food in his belly. Then to learn of the mass of debts Denis had left behind. It was like being at sea, battered by constant storms.

There had been a momentary easing that afternoon, with Cadence's ability to charm Antony Wigton, and Wigton's promise to help them out of this dilemma. But now this summons from Quinn.

It couldn't be good. His dispatch from the Foreign Office had been genteel, with iron beneath the words. He would not be welcome there any longer.

Joe appeared at the door to the office. "Mr. Wigton is here," he said.

"Show him into the parlor, Joe," Reed said. "And then run up to Lady Harlow's room and notify her."

He met Wigton in the parlor. "I thought the Countess of Harlow could use some help with answering the condolence notes she has received," Wigton said. "I know you and your sister are not quite as familiar with London standards."

"That's very kind of you, Wigton," Reed said. "Though I'm not sure our funds will stretch to that kind of service."

The Lord's Gambit

"Please, consider it a professional courtesy," Wigton said. "After all the loss your family has endured, it would be unconscionable to charge for such a basic assistance." He hesitated, then added, "These social forms can be quite demanding, especially in times of grief. I would be honored to help guide Lady Harlow through them."

"We appreciate your help," Reed said. "We are both country born and bred, and my time in the Navy did not lend to social graces. Cadence has been an excellent student of social mores since her season, and her marriage, but both of us are unfamiliar with the responses for notes of condolence."

"It is my pleasure to help," Wigton said. "Though I am a country boy myself, I learned a great deal in my time at the bar, and now as a solicitor. One of my housemates is a second son to a baron and he lost his father last year, so I am quite familiar with these things."

Cadence approached, her movements measured. Wigton's eyes met hers, and for a moment, something unspoken passed between them—a recognition that transcended the formal constraints of the moment. He shifted slightly, creating space for her while maintaining proper distance, and inclined his head in a gesture that was both deferential and deeply personal. When Mrs. Clarkson entered with the tea, Wigton's fingers brushed the sleeve of his waistcoat, a gesture that seemed to steady himself more than adjust his clothing.

Reed noted the connection between the two of them, and was pleased that his friend was able to connect with his sister. He left them in the parlor and returned to the office with his teacup and a biscuit, and as he nibbled and drank he thought about Quinn's summons. His work at the Foreign Office had been thorough, he knew. He reviewed and summarized documents, provided advice, and conducted correspondence. He went over each of the major projects he had worked on, and could not recall any that might have created cause for alarm months later.

Finally, he gave up. Through the open door of the parlor, Reed observed Wigton and Cadence at the small table, their heads close together over the condolence letters. When Wigton demonstrated the proper way to fold the black-bordered paper, their fingers brushed. His sister's breath caught audibly, and Wigton's hand trembled as he withdrew it.

"My apologies, Lady Harlow," he murmured, but his eyes lingered on her face.

"No need," Cadence replied softly. "Your guidance is most... appreciated."

Reed saw the way Wigton's expression softened, how Cadence's cheeks colored prettily. Even in her widow's weeds, she seemed to glow in Wigton's presence.

He went back into the office, and remembered a lecturer at Repton who had said, "There is no past and no future. There is only today, and you must make the most of it."

Not exactly a motto for the Foreign Office, which dealt equally in the actions of the past, the problems of the present, and fears for the future. But it was good advice for him that Monday afternoon. Focus only on moving forward from day to day.

He had faith that Antony Wigton would help Cadence sort through the maze of her inheritance, and that there would be enough money to pay off Denis's debts and set Cadence up in a new situation. He was relieved as well that Wigton had made no mention of his disgrace.

He spent some time that afternoon in the library. As she got older, his mother had taken to stashing the odd banknote in unusual places, like between the leaves of a romance novel or at the back of the bread box.

He opened book after book, often flushing out notes in the hand of the 5th Earl or his predecessors, but no money. Then something caught his eye, a small leather volume about the British railway system. Inside the front cover was a notation in Denis's hand: "Follow the money through Budapest. Professor V knows more than he claims."

Reed tucked the book into his pocket, thinking he might examine it more closely later. But for now, his thoughts kept returning to

Quinn's summons. What could the Foreign Office want with him, after the circumstances of his departure? He could think of nothing that would warrant this meeting.

By the time Wigton left and Mrs. Clarkson served dinner, Reed forced himself to eat, though his appetite had deserted him. Sleep would likely prove just as elusive, with tomorrow's meeting with Quinn weighing on his mind.

Chapter 12
A Small Error
Israel

Tuesday morning Israel looked at himself in the mirror. Shaving his beard and payess made him look younger, especially as he had lost so much weight that his face was gaunt. Ezra had taken him to an outfitter's shop in Hackney on Saturday morning, and bought him two sets of clothes. "You are bound to grow larger once we have you fed," Ezra said. "Don't want to waste money on clothes that won't fit you for much longer."

In the end, the outfitter had adjusted shirts and trousers from a larger size, so that Israel could simply slice through seams as he grew stouter. But before he could dress for work with Silas, he began with his undershorts and then his tzitzit. That was a simple, rectangular garment made of lightweight white cotton, resembling a sleeveless undershirt.

What made it distinctive were the four corners, each adorned with carefully knotted fringes or tassels made of white threads. These fringes, commanded by Jewish law, hung down from each corner, a constant reminder of God's commandments. As Israel slipped it over his head, he felt the familiar brush of the soft cotton against his skin and the gentle weight of the tassels at his sides, a tangible connection to his faith that he maintained even as other aspects of his appearance changed.

He pulled on a pair of the new trousers and tucked the tassels into the waistband. The white shirt had a higher collar than he was accustomed to but the single-breasted dark sack coat hung correctly to his hip, without a defined waist.

Ezra had bought him a solid pair of leather shoes and a leather belt as well. When he was satisfied with the way he looked, he walked out of his room.

"You look like a proper clerk," Ezra said, as Israel met him in the hallway.

"Do you think Silas's barrister will take me on? I did help my uncle with his bookkeeping, but I have no training in that field."

"I've never spoken to Silas about how he learned his craft, but there's nothing to say that you can't qualify as Luke did."

Silas came downstairs a moment later and cast an appraising eye on Israel. "I suppose you will do," he said. "Come along, we have a walk ahead of us."

"I have told you that you can afford the streetcar," Ezra said.

"And I take advantage of that, at the end of the day. In the morning I find a brisk walk sets me up quite well."

Ezra's home was on the south side of Hackney, close to the Regent Canal, and as they crossed the bridge over that waterway, Israel could hold out no longer. "Do you think Mr. Pemberton will accept me?" he asked.

"Our office has a problem. We need someone capable of analyzing bills and creating a record of them. If you can solve that problem, Mr. Pemberton will be happy with you."

Silas took a deep breath. "Richard Pemberton is a fair man who judges people on their abilities, not their background. But his standards are exacting."

Israel turned to look at him. "What you mean?"

"He expects his employees to work hard and maintain proper

professional standards at all times. But if you can do that, he will treat you well."

Israel nodded. "And is there anyone else in the office?"

"The assistant clerk, Luke. He is very young, barely out of his teens, though he is proving to be quite smart. And Robb is only a boy, and a very boyish one at that."

They followed Queensbridge Road in silence for some time. As they walked, Silas pirouetted gracefully around each puddle, protecting his immaculate boots. He paused to adjust the lay of his coat, cut precisely to emphasize his slim waist, and straightened the jet buttons that marched down his chest. Even in this early hour, every detail of his appearance was perfect.

Israel spent the rest of the walk in wide-eyed amazement. The buildings were larger, the streets cleaner, and there were flowers around the trees. If all this was just a few blocks' walk from where he had lived, what else was out there?

He followed Silas down Chancery Lane, past a gatehouse with an elaborate coat of arms. "That is the Great Hall over there," Silas said. "That building with high ceilings, intricate wooden carvings, and large stained-glass window. Our office is ahead of us, on the second floor of a building overlooking the Old Square."

"It is very impressive," Israel said in a small voice.

"And meant to be," Silas said. "This is the home of British justice."

They were the first to arrive. "I'm not sure where you will sit," Silas said. "You may hang your coat and hat beside mine. Once you have met Mr. Pemberton, and he approves, you will accompany me to Somerset House, where we will search for estate records."

Silas busied himself lighting the gas lamps and boiling water for tea, and eventually the two other junior members of the staff arrived. Luke was a handsome Irish lad, tall and lanky, with a shaft of blond hair and piercing blue eyes. Robb was younger, shorter and darker.

It was clear that Silas was in charge. He assigned duties to both the boys, and gave Israel the accounts book he used. "If you can make sense of that, you can do the job," he said.

Israel sat on a chair on the other side of Silas's desk and began to look at the entries. He was relieved to see that he understood them completely. He redid the math as he went, and he was surprised to find a small error. Should he point it out? What if Silas was angry?

He steeled himself. "Excuse me, Silas," he said.

Silas looked up. "You don't understand something?"

"I think I find an error in math," he said timidly. He turned the book around so that Silas could see. "On line 12."

Silas grabbed a slate and chalk and redid the sum. Then he looked up at Israel. "You did this in your head?"

Israel nodded.

"You have identified a calculation error on my part. I appreciate your thoroughness. I shall have to adjust the client's bill."

They both went back to work, and then the door swept open and Richard Pemberton walked in. Though well into his forties, Pemberton was a commanding figure, carrying his weight with the dignity of success. "You must be our new bookkeeper," he said, reaching out to shake Israel's hand.

"If you approve," Silas said. He rose to greet Pemberton, pausing to adjust his perfectly starched collar and smooth the sleeves of his plum-colored coat. A silk handkerchief peeked from his breast pocket, precisely arranged to show three points, and his watch chain gleamed against his waistcoat.

"I trust your opinion completely," Pemberton said. He turned to Israel once more. "You will learn quickly that our senior clerk is extremely qualified. Do not hesitate to ask him any questions you have."

"Thank you, sir. I appreciate chance to work here."

Pemberton laughed. "Let's see if you say that on Friday afternoon." Then he walked into his office.

"You and I will work out the details," Silas said to Israel. Then he stood. "For now, let us go to Somerset House and begin our research."

Chapter 13
Foreign Office
Reed

Tuesday morning Reed arrived at the Foreign Office, where he had worked for two years before being dismissed. He hesitated at the entrance to the glorious lobby with its inlaid blue tile floor and the expansive arched loggias on each floor. He'd once belonged here, a cog in the wheel that kept his nation moving. Now what was he?

He checked with a bowler-hatted porter and was directed to the top floor. The man's stoic face revealed nothing of whether he recognized Reed or remembered his name, and that was fine with him.

Men moved quickly past him with the efficiency of those on whose shoulders the fate of the nation rested. Fortunately, he did not recognize any of them. He climbed the stairs to Quinn's office, where the man sat with his back to a window overlooking the street. He was of a height with Reed, though his years behind a desk had led him to put on a few pounds since the last time they'd met.

Reed stood before Quinn, acutely aware of how his past decisions and the circumstances of his dismissal had led him to this moment. Quinn didn't rise to shake his hand, merely motioned him to the chair across from him. "I understand you have been living with your sister, the Countess of Harlow," he said.

Reed put on his most brittle persona. "That's correct. It has been difficult to gain reasonable employment since... my departure from these offices. Without college behind me, and under the situation of my dismissal... well, you must understand."

"I do. And I regret the circumstances, but they are neither here nor there. I have a problem I must address, and I think you are the right man for the job."

Reed's heart leapt in his chest like a trout on a line. "A job?" he asked.

"Nothing long-term, you understand, though it might be a way to claw yourself back into good graces. I need you to examine your late brother-in-law's finances."

"You know about the debts?" Reed asked. He couldn't imagine why the Foreign Office would be concerned with Cadence's financial situation.

"In a very general way. Your brother-in-law was quite a profligate gambler. Did you know that?"

"I knew he spent time in gaming hells," Reed said. "But it was not my business to inquire about the money he spent or lost there. That is, until he passed and left a mess for my sister to clean up."

"Has the name Sergei Litvinov come up as you have cleaned?"

Reed shook his head. "We only became aware of the depth of the problem on Saturday. We have engaged a firm of solicitors to clarify Cadence's situation."

"That is where I need you to step in," Quinn said. "This Litvinov has been working his way into polite society through his presence in various gaming hells. He finds a good prospect, one with a title and some illiquid assets, and establishes a connection, lending money to cover debts."

"A predatory lender?" Reed asked. "Extortionate interest and so on?"

Quinn nodded. "Often debts may be repaid by strategic votes in the House of Lords."

"But isn't that traitorous behavior?"

"It is. And sometimes, a man of honor may resort to other means to satisfy his debts. Such as suicide."

"I would hardly call Lord Harlow a man of honor," Reed said. "But perhaps you are right. Do you believe that he killed himself to avoid paying this Litvinov, or voting his way in the House of Lords?"

"It's a possibility. But right now all I have are rumors that Harlow owed Litvinov. As you can imagine, such debts are not recorded anywhere other than by borrower and lender."

"And these debts aren't legally enforceable in court, are they?" Reed asked.

"You're correct. Under the Gaming Act of 1845, all contracts or agreements related to gaming or wagering are null and void. Gaming, however, incurs a debt of honor. Failure to pay could result in social ostracism or being barred from clubs. Which might have been a motivating factor in Lord Harlow's decision to commit suicide."

"I still don't understand why this is a concern of the Foreign Office."

"While the debt itself can't be enforced, checks or IOUs given to cover gambling debts may be enforced as separate contracts. That's where Sergei Litvinov comes in. He takes a gambler's IOU, and then tears it up once the gambler has complied with Litvinov's requirements."

Reed nodded.

"As you know, the Russian Empire is our primary rival in The Great Game, our strategic rivalry over Central Asia. It is our fear that Litvinov is exploiting tensions over Russian expansion towards India. By manipulating votes in the House of Lords, he may be able to sway policy in Russia's favor."

"But now that Lord Harlow is dead, he can do no harm."

"That is true. But if we can expose a connection between Harlow and Litvinov, we can issue a warning to other members of the gentry. Don't deal with Litvinov or any of his agents."

"I see. And you need proof of that connection."

"Yes. And you are in the perfect position to provide it. Work with this solicitor's office, and keep your eye out for Litvinov." He pushed a sheet of paper over the desk toward Reed, who picked it up. "Those are the company names we know that Litvinov uses for his loan work. Of course there may be others, so you should be on the lookout for them."

"As you pointed out, we will be incurring expenses for a clerk and a bookkeeper, which we have engaged through Blackwood, Finch & Hartley," Reed said. "Would those be reimbursed from her Majesty's coffers?"

"We would prefer to keep this agreement under wraps. So I propose that we rehire you on temporary terms, at your previous salary, until this situation is resolved. Whatever your sister cannot pay of the bill from the solicitors will be your responsibility to pay from that salary."

It was better than Reed could have hoped for.

"I am glad to be of service to her Majesty again," he said. "How much of this can I share with our solicitor, Antony Wigton?"

"Let's keep the Foreign Office out of this research until we can confirm that Lord Harlow was indeed indebted to Sergei Litvinov or one of his affiliates. We pay you, you and your sister pay the solicitors."

"I will have to confer with my sister, but I am sure she will see the importance of cooperation."

"Excellent. Keep in touch, and treat this matter with the utmost urgency. There are bills pending in the House of Lords which Litvinov may seek to influence."

Reed left, stumbling on his way through the blue-tiled lobby as his brain rushed to make sense of everything he had learned that morning. First he would have to meet with Cadence and let her into the secrets. Then he had to address Antony Wigton and inform him that he would be part of the research team.

It seemed simple, but he was sure it would become complicated quickly.

Chapter 14
Somerset House
Silas

Silas once again led Israel, this time through the early spring morning to Somerset House, an impressive neoclassical building. The south face, overlooking the Thames, was a light, creamy stone with a symmetrical design of a central block and two flanking wings. The river front was adorned with columns, statues, and intricate stonework.

"This is Somerset House," he said. "The home of the Principal Probate Registry. Wills and probate records may be searched here."

From the Strand, they entered the building's large central courtyard, and then the main door, passing clerks and attorneys coming and going. The grand entrance hall was bustling as well, and the high ceilings and well-dressed men around him made Silas feel small and insignificant.

If he felt that way, then Israel probably felt worse, so he put a hand on the man's shoulder in reassurance. If Israel was to be Ezra's puppy dog, and work with Silas, then it was incumbent on him to treat the man well, despite any fears he might have that Israel would seek to replace him in Ezra's bed.

He found his way to the Probate Registry, which was lit by a mixture of gas lamps and natural light from the large windows. He and Israel waited until there was a clerk free.

"I am here under the auspices of Blackwood, Finch & Hartley. Our firm represents the Countess Harlow, widow of the sixth Earl of Harlow. We are researching the conditions of the title and the affiliated property, and would like to see all documents relating to the estate of James Greenwood, the fifth Earl of Harlow."

He also provided the date and location of the man's death.

"I have to check the Calendar of Wills," the clerk said. "I will be back."

As the clerk moved farther into the room, Silas whispered, "That is an index of probate records organized by year and alphabetically by the deceased's surname."

Once the clerk found the right listing and confirmed it with Silas, Silas requested to see the will and affiliated probate documents. He paid the appropriate fee and received a receipt for Pemberton. The clerk took down his request and then moved to an area of cabinets and shelves.

Despite the archive's dusty atmosphere, Silas maintained his pristine appearance, constantly brushing his sleeves with a small ivory-backed brush he produced from his pocket. His cuffs, secured with silver links shaped like butterflies, remained crisp and white. Even his hair stayed perfectly arranged, unlike the disheveled clerks around them.

While they waited, Silas looked around at the clerks fulfilling other requests, and he felt reassured. He was part of this grand process. "Small steps," he said to Israel. "Let me tell you a bit about the men around us."

"Please do."

"The barristers usually only wear their wigs in the courtroom," Silas said, "though some of the men around us are probably barristers on a brief break between cases, without time to return to their offices. Those gowns they wear are black silk. You'll see Mr. Pemberton dress that way when he has to go to court."

"I am sure he is quite a distinguished figure."

"He is. Now the men in the smart suits are usually solicitors, like Antony Wigton, who we will be working closely with." Many of the men around him wore knee-length frock coats, fitted at the waist and flaring out below. Whether double-breasted or single-breasted, they had wide lapels and decorative buttons.

"The clerks like us are the easiest to identify," Silas said. "Sack coats, much less formal, and more likely purchased at provisioners than from custom tailors." He lowered his voice. "You can spot many a frayed cuff or collar on men who spend their time peering down at documents."

It didn't take long for the clerk to find the records regarding the death of the elder Lord Harlow. He brought them a file folder of documents, and directed them to the reading room to review them. The reading room had a high ceiling and tall windows, and was full of tables and chairs, many of them occupied by clerks. The area was quiet and studious, and Silas imagined this was what it must be like for those who were fortunate enough to attend a university.

He found them both seats at a large table and opened the folder he'd been given. He began reading the will, while he passed the list of assets to Israel to evaluate.

Lord James Harlow's will left the bulk of his worldly goods to his only son, Denis Greenwood, who was to succeed him to the title of Lord Harlow. Subject, of course, to the restrictions of his title.

He quickly realized that it was going to take a lot of time to review everything in the folder, and that eventually he was going to have to trace the title back until it was granted to fully understand what the ramifications were of the Earl's death.

He went back to the clerk and asked for those records. "It will take some time to recall them from the archives," the clerk said. He scribbled out a ticket and handed it to Silas. "You'll have to come back in two hours. Use this ticket to claim them."

Silas thanked him and returned to the reading room, where the chandeliers and extensive paneling spoke volumes about the commerce conducted therein. He and Israel read and took notes, reviewing small legacies to staff and distant relations. There was also a codicil to the will which identified the properties the Lord owned in Gloucestershire, including Drayton House, the family seat. Drawings were attached which indicated the boundaries of the land owned by Lord Harlow. They included a half-dozen tenant farmers, a stable, an orchard, an icehouse, a mill, and a dovecote.

There was a home farm, directly managed by the estate, pastures for livestock and arable land for crops. A river formed one edge of the property, and fishing rights had been granted to several tenants. There was also a small woodland, with the right to harvest timber granted to another tenant.

Adjacent to one field, which had been reserved for the grazing of milk cows, was a dairy, which produced cheese. On the other side of the dairy was a small village, where the cottages were owned by the Earl and rented out to his workers.

It looked quite profitable to Silas, and he hoped that the information on the title itself would reveal that it passed on to the Countess, rather than that cousin who inherited the title. If the Countess was lucky, her husband's title was a dry or titular one, not connected to the land around Drayton Manor. Then she would have the means to pay off her husband's creditors, even if it took a while, and to pay for the work done by Antony Wigton's firm, and himself.

But as Silas gathered their papers to leave, a single sheet fluttered to the floor. He bent to retrieve it and noticed something odd. The letterhead identified it as from somewhere called The Gilded Serpent, with a serpentine emblem.

It was a receipt listing "consulting fees" paid to a man named Colin Sinclair, signed by Denis Greenwood, Lord Harlow, with the initials DG scrawled beside the signature.

"Another piece to add to the puzzle," Silas murmured, tucking the paper into his folder. They'd have to wait to see all the records to understand how these fragments fit together.

Chapter 15
Sergei Litvinov
Reed

Reed was happy to find Cadence dressed and reading through papers in Denis's office when he returned to Bloomsbury Square late on Tuesday afternoon. "What did they want from you at the Foreign Office?" she asked. "It must be something good, because you are smiling."

"It is, dear sister. Better than I could have expected." He explained that he was being given a temporary position, at his previous salary.

"To do what?"

"To do exactly what you and I have been doing. To examine Denis's debts. Have you ever heard of a man called Sergei Litvinov?"

"A Russian? No, I don't think I have."

"It seems Denis racked up significant gambling debts. The good news is that those debts cannot be enforced against you in a court of law."

"That is a relief."

"However, there is bad news as well. It appears that Denis borrowed money from lenders to pay off his gambling losses. Those debts are enforceable."

Cadence sagged against her chair. "Do we know how much is involved?"

Reed shook his head. "That is what I will have to research. Hopefully with the help of the bookkeeper Wigton will employ. I am to keep this Russian's name out of it as much as possible, as well as the involvement of the Foreign Office. But I must go to Wigton's office this afternoon and let him know that there may be markers out there with Denis's name on them."

"How will you find out what he owed?"

"I shall have to visit the gambling hells he frequented. See what he owed to the management, and what they can tell me about anyone else who might have purchased his markers."

"This is all very frightening," Cadence said. "I don't know what to think, or what to worry about next."

"If most of Denis's property passes to that cousin who becomes the seventh earl, then I hope the debts will transfer as well. Which would leave you impoverished, but at least not at risk of bankruptcy."

"And what if it doesn't?"

"Then we will have the income from the estate to apply against the debts. That's something I will work on with the bookkeeper."

Cadence began to cry, and Reed moved over to sit beside her and put his arm around her shoulders. "Whatever we must face, we will face together," he said. "You have been good to me in my time of trouble, so I will stand by you."

What he did not wish to remind his sister was that if she went down, he would go down with her. If neither of them had money, he would have to get a job somewhere, even if just as a clerk, and they would lose the house on Bloomsbury Square and anything they owned that had value, including the pearls Denis had given her as a wedding gift.

He squeezed her shoulder. They had come into the world as siblings, and would continue together.

"And now, let us see what Mrs. Clarkson has put together for lunch," Reed said. "I shall need to be fortified to venture back to Wigton's office."

They ate, and Cadence seemed to feel better after Mrs. Clarkson's pigeon pie.

He set out for Lincoln's Inn Fields after they finished eating. He handed his card to the clerk, who sent him upstairs on his own to Wigton's office.

As Wigton had said, his office was a small one, crammed with law books and paper files. His diploma from Cambridge hung on the wall.

"Ah, Lydney, I'm glad you dropped by," Wigton said, rising to shake Reed's hand. "I have good news to share."

He motioned Reed to the wooden chair across from his desk, and they both sat. "I often work in tandem with a barrister called Richard Pemberton. I spent some time in his office after I finished my studies. He has an excellent clerk he can lend us, and this clerk, Silas by name, has managed to rustle up a bookkeeper to help."

"That is good news," Reed said.

"I will go over there tomorrow morning. Silas is at Somerset House today, researching the wills of the various Lord Harlows, to get a better sense of your sister's situation."

"There's something you should know," Reed said. "This morning the Foreign Office asked me to look into Denis's affairs. I can't say more than that, but I'd appreciate your discretion in the matter."

Wigton's eyebrows rose slightly, but he nodded. "Of course. I understand completely."

Reed agreed to meet with Wigton the next morning, and returned to Bloomsbury Square, where he found Cadence in the parlor, working through the pile of condolence notes. "Has Wigton been of service to you in this regard?" he asked.

She smiled, and Reed felt his heart lighten. "He has. I still will need advice with several of these, but I understand how to answer the bulk of them."

Reed knew that he needed to keep Cadence engaged, keep giving her a reason to rise and dress each morning. "What say you accompany me tomorrow to meet Pemberton and Silas and this bookkeeper. We can see what they have learned."

"If you wish," Cadence said. "Do you think Antony Wigton will be there?"

Reed noted her smile. "I think it's entirely possible. And we need to meet with him again soon anyway."

A slight blush rose to Cadence's cheek, and Reed smiled to see it.

Chapter 16
Introductions
Israel

"This is it!" Silas said to Israel late on Tuesday afternoon. "I've found the original grant to the very first Lord Harlow."

Israel moved closer to Silas to look at the document with him. "There is no mention here of entailment," Silas said, with pleasure.

"What does that mean, exactly?" Israel asked.

"The landed gentry often use what is called a fee tail to preserve family estates across generations. Usually it means that the property can only be inherited by specific heirs, most often the eldest male descendant. That is a problem when a member of the gentry only has daughters, and so he has no money to leave directly to them."

Israel nodded.

"The current holder of the estate is called the tenant-in-tail and can't sell the property or leave it to someone else in their will, without an act of Parliament, which is very difficult to obtain. Because there is no entailment, that means Lady Harlow can inherit her husband's properties." He smiled. "And have the money to pay us to organize her late husband's debts."

"That is good, right?"

"Very good. Let's make a few more notes and then we will head back to Hackney. Tomorrow morning we will pass on this good news to Pemberton and Wigton."

"In the Torah, there is story that reminds me of this entailment you speak about," Israel said. "It's in the book of Numbers, chapter 27. The daughters of Zelophehad come to Moses because their father dies without sons. They ask, 'Why should our father's name disappear from his clan because he has no son? Give us property among our father's relatives.'"

"Interesting," Silas said. "I have very little knowledge of the Bible. What does Moses say?"

"Moses asks the Lord for advice, and the Lord says 'What Zelophehad's daughters are saying is right. You must give them property as an inheritance among their father's relatives and give their father's inheritance to them.'"

"That is very good," Silas said.

"It makes a new law in Israel. If a man dies without a son, his inheritance go to his daughter. Only if he has no children at all does it go to other relatives." Israel leaned forward. "Your people say they follow the Bible, but maybe they do not know this section."

Silas was impressed with Israel's knowledge, and his ability to connect their case to what he had studied. Perhaps he would be able to contribute more than just a head for numbers.

That evening at dinner, Silas was eager to share the progress they had made with Ezra, and he included the connection that Israel had made.

Ezra beamed. "I am proud of you, Israel," he said. "Look at how much progress you have made in only a few days. We will make a proper Englishman of you soon!"

"But what of the Ragged School?" Israel asked. "The children..."

"This work with the solicitors is more important," Ezra said. "Though perhaps, when things settle, you could come teach special lessons now and then. The children would benefit from your gift with numbers."

For the first time in many days, Israel slept soundly that night, and awakened with joy to the morning light.

He and Silas walked briskly to Gray's Inn on Wednesday morning. Israel was proud of the way he looked, like many other men on the street. He even walked differently, keeping up with Silas's stride. He was a man of importance, however small, due at an office where his work was valued.

As soon as he and Silas hung up their coats, they prepared a brief report for Richard Pemberton, who was in court that morning with Antony Wigton on a case. By the time Pemberton and Wigton returned to the office, they had summarized their results.

Luke made everyone tea, and they sat in Pemberton's office. But before they could get started, the front door opened and a man and woman stepped in. Israel looked out and was stunned to recognize the man who had been so kind to him on that wintry day, when he was at his lowest. Reed Lydney.

Who was the woman with him, though? His wife? She was as beautiful as he was handsome, the same blonde hair and widely spaced eyes.

Every detail of their conversation was etched in his mind. He had a sister, didn't he? Had Reed ever mentioned her name? He stared wide-eyed at the pair of them as he struggled to recall. Yes, their father had been an amateur musician, and given them musical names. Reed was a kind of instrument, and Cadence a measure of rhythm.

All four men stood to greet the newcomers, and Israel was so distracted he nearly toppled his chair.

"Ah, Lydney," Wigton said. "And the lovely Countess of Harlow." He sketched a quick bow. "Let me introduce you."

He did so, and Israel saw Reed's eyes widen as he heard Israel's name. Did he have as strong a memory of that day as Israel did? From the way he gripped his hands together, as if to hold back from reaching out, Israel thought he might.

Chapter 17
Path through the Forest
Reed

Reed was stunned to realize that the bookkeeper was the very same man he had met earlier that winter. It was as if a fairy godmother had come in and completely made him over, though the dark eyes and full mouth remained the same, allowing his inner beauty to shine that much more.

He was struck with the memory of their encounter, and the connection they had felt. He had even passed by that street several times, on the lookout for the ragged man who shared his love of poetry. And now to be thrown together!

But he could not reveal their connection, not to his sister or the attorneys or anyone else. Not until he had had a chance to speak directly with Israel.

A boy brought two more chairs into Pemberton's office, and it was a tight fit for all of them. Reed found himself sitting very closely to Israel, trying desperately to keep from sharing glances.

Fortunately, Israel was absorbed by the information he and Silas had to present. When Silas announced that there was no entailment on Denis's estate, Reed sighed deeply and clutched Cadence's hand. She was overcome, and used her free hand to wipe away tears.

"This is excellent news," Wigton said. "I feel like we have been walking through a forest, and a path ahead has suddenly appeared."

"It is very good news," Pemberton said. "Congratulations on your excellent research, Silas."

"Israel was very helpful in reading the documents," Silas said, and Reed felt himself unaccountably happy about that.

"But this is only the first step on that path," Pemberton continued. "Wigton, what should we focus on next?"

"We need a complete accounting of the late Lord Harlow's debts, as well as of the assets of his estate."

Reed was surprised when Cadence spoke up. "My brother and I have been hard at work assembling all the bills we have record of," she said. She opened her tapestry purse and withdrew several folded sheets of paper, which she handed to Wigton.

As she did, once again Reed observed the lingering touch of their fingers, the way his old school friend's face softened when he looked at her. These small gestures confirmed what Reed had already begun to suspect from Wigton's eagerness to help with the condolence letters. His interest in Cadence went beyond mere professional courtesy.

Reed watched as she smiled and looked down at her lap, a becoming blush coloring her cheeks. She was beautiful and charming, and clearly Wigton was not immune to those charms. But was it proper to encourage such attention so soon after Denis's death? Even if Wigton's intentions were honorable?

Gods, was his interest in Israel as blatant as hers in Wigton? He hoped not!

Wigton took the papers and scanned them, then handed them across the desk to Silas. "These look very comprehensive," he said.

"I am given to understand that Denis also had gambling debts," Reed said. "Which are not represented there. I am not sure how we would go about discovering them."

"Do you know which hell he frequented?" Wigton asked.

Reed looked at Cadence. "Did he ever mention one?"

She shook her head. But then she reached into her purse again and pulled out the chip they had found among Denis's effects. "Does this mean anything?"

Once again she handed it to Wigton, and once again they both smiled as their hands met. "One of the men I share lodgings with, another solicitor, has a taste for gambling hells, and I recognize the logo here," Wigton said. "It comes from The Gilded Serpent."

"That does not sound pleasant," Cadence said.

Wigton laughed. "Depending on your interests, it could be quite a welcoming place."

"Then I should go there tonight," Reed said. "And inquire about Denis."

Cadence put her hand on his arm. "Do you think that wise?"

"I am not as innocent as I might seem," Reed said. "While I have never been to a gambling hell, I did serve two years in her Majesty's Navy. I am able to comport myself in various situations."

"I should accompany you," Wigton said. "Strength in numbers and all that, right? Shall I come to Bloomsbury Square at nine this evening?"

"I welcome your company," Reed said.

"We found something relevant in the paperwork at Somerset House," Silas said. He passed the paper with the Gilded Serpent logo to Wigton.

"Yes, this is the place," Wigton said. "Though I do not recognize the name of Colin Sinclair."

"Another gambler, perhaps?" Reed asked.

"We can ask this evening," Wigton said.

Pemberton laid out the remaining tasks. "Next, we shall need to establish what properties remain in the estate, and what income can be expected of them. Do you have such records at your disposal?" he asked Reed.

"We have some," Reed said. And then, emboldened, he added, "Perhaps Mr. Kupersmit could come to Bloomsbury Square and help me sort through the records?"

Pemberton looked to Israel, whose face flushed. "I am honored," he said.

"Excellent," Pemberton said. "Our first steps through the forest have been mapped out. And now, if the rest of you will excuse us, Mr. Wigton and I must discuss a different case."

Everyone rose, and after much shaking of hands, Silas returned to his desk, and Wigton closed the door to Pemberton's office. That left Reed, Cadence, and Israel standing awkwardly together.

"We will need a carriage to return to Bloomsbury Square," Reed said, and the boy, whose name was Robb, volunteered to hail one. The three of them followed him outside.

"It is most kind of you to come with us," Cadence said. "Did I discern that you have a previous acquaintance? I felt some connection between you."

"A cup of tea on a cold day," Reed said. "We met on the street and discovered a common love of the poetry of Keats, and repaired inside to discuss it. Unfortunately we have not seen each other since."

"Well, this will give you a chance to renew your friendship," Cadence said, as a carriage pulled up.

Chapter 18
Paperwork
Israel

Israel waited as Reed helped his sister into the carriage, and then took a seat across from her. Reed moved aside so that Israel could squeeze in beside him. He was acutely aware of the Reed's presence against him, the way that Reed's knee shook slightly against his own.

Every time the carriage rocked over cobblestones, Israel and Reed were pushed together. Israel was embarrassed at the way his cock reacted, but then he looked down at Reed's lap and saw the same situation. He could only hope that Reed sister was too innocent to notice.

But she had been married, so she must have had some knowledge of men and the way they reacted to stimuli. He forced himself to look out the window as London passed by. Ladies with tiny reticules hung from their wrists and errand boys carrying packages. A bobby with a tall hard helmet covered in blue serge stood on a street corner, wearing a dark blue frock coat with silver buttons.

A month ago, he would have shivered in horror at the sight of a bobby, fearing a kick from his heavy ankle-high leather boots or a rap from the truncheon he carried in a leather holster. It was hard to realize how far he had come in so short a time. Now he was riding in a carriage like a respectable person, headed to a home he would never have dared enter.

He was relieved when the carriage pulled up in front of a three-story home with a flat roof. It was so much more elegant than the simple home where he was staying with Ezra, and after he jumped out of the carriage he stood there admiring it.

The stucco coating was a pale yellow, with large sash windows with multiple panes on the front, becoming slightly smaller on the upper floors. A short flight of stone steps led to the front door, which was solid wood, painted black, with a fanlight above.

Reed stepped out of the carriage and helped his sister alight, then paid the driver. Cadence walked up to the gate on the iron railing that enclosed a small front area and unlatched it. "Come in, please," she said to Israel.

He followed her up to the door, which she unlocked with a key that hung from her belt in what he had learned was called a chatelaine.

Israel followed her into the entry hallway. "Mrs. Clarkson, we have returned," Cadence called toward the kitchen. But no servants arrived to take their coats, so he helped Cadence with her cloak. "I'm afraid we have little staff," Cadence said as Reed joined them. "But if you wish tea, Mrs. Clarkson can provide it."

"I'll take Israel into his lordship's office and get him started," Reed said. "Tea can follow."

He felt Reed's hand on his arm. "This way," he said, and directed Israel into a room full of heavy wood furniture, dominated by a massive desk. Piles of paperwork were neatly assembled on its top.

Once they were alone with the door closed, Reed turned to him. "How did you end up at Pemberton's office? The last time we met you were... in a very different sort of employ."

Israel's face warmed at the memory. "After that day, Louise dismiss me. Say I not bring enough customers. I sleep on street until Ezra find me at Ragged School, where he teach boxing to poor children. He and Silas take me in, give me place to sleep. Then Silas see I am good with numbers and bring me to Pemberton."

"Ezra Curiel? The boxer?" Reed asked. In a moment he understood a great deal. Of course he'd heard of Curiel's scandal and his step away from boxing. And from what Israel had said, he and Silas lived together. It was as if a whole world had opened up in front of him. "So much has changed for you," he said softly.

"Yes. But one thing not change." Israel met Reed's eyes. "I never forget your kindness that day. The tea, the poetry, the way you see me as person, not just poor foreigner."

Reed walked to the chair behind the desk and settled, while pointing Israel to the chair beside him. "And now here you are, helping to solve my family's difficulties. Perhaps Providence had a hand in our meeting after all."

Israel smiled. He felt the same way about God's hand in his life. Perhaps he had been led through those difficulties in order to find his way here.

"I am glad of any help you can provide," Reed said. He handed Israel a stack of paper. "You may find some bills of sale in there for properties Denis sold."

Israel's fingers trembled slightly as he leafed through the stack of papers. The room was warm, stuffy with the scent of old books and leather, and he was acutely aware of Reed's presence beside him. The man's cologne, a subtle blend of sandalwood and citrus, was distracting in close quarters.

Then his search was rewarded. "I find another deed of sale," Israel said, holding up a document. "It look like Denis sell small farm in Gloucestershire last year."

Reed leaned in to examine the paper, his shoulder brushing against Israel's. The contact, brief as it was, sent a shiver down Israel's spine. "Good work," Reed said, his voice low. "Begin a list of sold properties. There is paper and a pen over there."

Israel nodded, trying to focus on the task at hand rather than the warmth radiating from Reed's body. He began the list, his usually neat handwriting slightly shaky.

"What you think about all this?" Israel asked, gesturing at the piles of documents surrounding them. "It seem Denis sell many things."

Reed sighed, running a hand through his hair. The gesture drew Israel's eyes to the man's strong jawline, the way his shirt collar emphasized the elegant curve of his neck. "I think my brother-in-law was in deeper trouble than any of us realized," he said.

Israel nodded, then frowned as he examined another document. "This one I not understand," he said, holding it out to Reed. "Language is very... complex."

Reed took the paper, his fingers brushing against Israel's as he did so. The touch lingered a moment longer than necessary, and Israel felt his cheeks grow warm. Reed's brow furrowed as he read the document, and Israel found himself admiring the man's concentration, the intelligence evident in his clear blue eyes.

"This is interesting," Reed murmured. "It appears Denis still owned a small property in London. A townhouse in Mayfair. The address is not far from here."

He sat back. "I wonder if Denis kept a mistress there."

Israel stared at him in surprise. "You think that is possible?"

"Denis held so many secrets anything is possible."

"But finding this property is good news, yes?" Israel asked, leaning closer to look at the document. He could feel the heat of Reed's body, smell the faint traces of tobacco on his breath.

Reed nodded slowly. "It could be. We'll need to investigate further, see if there are any liens against it. And track if it is rented, and where that income is going."

Their eyes met, and for a moment, Israel forgot to breathe. There was something in Reed's gaze, a mixture of admiration and desire that made his heart race. But then Reed cleared his throat and looked away, the moment broken.

"We should... we should continue," Reed said, his voice slightly hoarse. "There's still much to go through."

Israel nodded, trying to ignore the pang of disappointment he felt. "Yes, you are right. We have much work to do."

As they returned to their task, Israel couldn't help but steal glances at Reed, wondering if the man felt the same tension, the same longing that he did. But such thoughts were dangerous, he knew. For now, he would focus on the work at hand, and try to ignore the way his heart leapt every time Reed's hand accidentally brushed against his own.

They worked for several hours. "I'm afraid we have kept you here longer than expected," Reed said. He looked closely at Israel. "You said you were staying with Silas and Ezra Curiel?"

Israel nodded. "Yes, they have offered me a room in their home in Hackney."

Their home, Reed heard. With what he knew of the boxer, and the way that Silas dressed, he understood what their relationship was.

"That is quite far from here. I'll call you a carriage."

"Oh, no. I walk. Is good for me."

Reed shook his head. "At least take a few pence for the omnibus. We don't have much, but I can spare that. You can catch one at the corner of the square which will take you to Liverpool Street, and transfer to another one to Hackney."

He dug in his pocket and handed a pair of tuppence to Israel. He took the coins, once again feeling a shiver as his fingers touched Reed's. "I teach these coins to children at the Ragged School," he said.

"Will you keep teaching there now that you are working for Pemberton?"

Israel shrugged. "I do what I need. Ezra is most generous and tells me to gain weight and grow stronger."

Israel remembered watching Ezra at the Ragged School the day before, how he'd hoisted three children at once on his broad shoulders, his boxer's strength controlled and gentle with the little ones.

He felt Reed's eyes on him. "Yes, you could do with more meat on your bones," he said.

There was an uncomfortable silence for a moment, and then Israel said, "I go now. I come back here tomorrow?"

"Yes, that would be good. You can tell Silas what you have done."

Israel stood, and Reed did also. Israel held out his hand for a shake, but he was stunned when Reed pulled him into an embrace. His whole body shivered at the connection, and he felt Reed react the same way. He inhaled Reed's cologne and felt a part of himself dissolving in the connection

"Thank you for everything," Reed said, when he pulled back. "I appreciate your help."

"I am the one who owe you the thanks," Israel said. "I hope my work will pay you back for your kindness."

"And I hope we will continue our association," Reed said.

Israel nodded shakily, and then turned for the door. He did not trust himself to say anything further.

Chapter 19
The Gilded Serpent
Reed

As promised, Antony Wigton arrived at Bloomsbury Square at nine that night to take Reed to Denis's favorite gambling hell. "Be careful," Cadence said.

"Don't worry, I will protect him," Wigton said, smiling at Cadence.

"I do not need protection," Reed protested. "Merely a guide through Hell. As Virgil did for Dante."

"A gentleman and a scholar," Wigton said, and they ventured out into the fog-shrouded night. Gas lamps cast dim halos in the mist as they made their way through London's fashionable quarter, their boots clicking against wet cobblestones. The respectable facades of St. James's Street gave way to shadowy passages between buildings, where less savory establishments conducted their business away from public view.

The Gilded Serpent occupied one such space. It was a notorious gambling hell located in a narrow alley that seemed designed for discretion. Its entrance was unmarked save for a small brass plaque bearing its serpentine emblem, tarnished by years of London smoke.

"I asked around this afternoon," Wigton said, as they approached the building. "It was established in 1845 by a retired naval officer with a penchant for high-stakes games. My understanding is that it is a favored haunt of the aristocracy and wealthy merchants seeking thrills beyond the staid gentleman's clubs of Pall Mall."

The building's upper windows were shuttered tight, though light leaked through the cracks, and the muffled sounds of masculine laughter drifted down to the street.

As Reed and Wigton approached the nondescript door, Reed felt a flutter of nervousness in his stomach. He had never visited such an establishment before, and the air of secrecy and vice made him uneasy. Wigton, however, seemed perfectly at ease as he rapped out a complex pattern on the door.

A small viewing slot slid open, and a pair of dark eyes peered out at them. "Sheffield arms," Wigton murmured, and the door swung open with a soft creak.

"The man who gave you this location also provided the password?" Reed asked in a low voice.

"Indeed," Wigton said, as he stepped forward.

The noise and smells hit Reed like a physical blow as they entered. The air was thick with tobacco smoke and the sharp scent of spirits, overlaid with the musty odor of sweat and desperation. The din of voices, punctuated by occasional shouts of triumph or groans of despair, created a cacophony that seemed to press in on all sides.

The entrance hall was dimly lit by gas lamps with red shades, casting an infernal glow over the proceedings. Plush red carpets muffled their footsteps as Wigton led the way deeper into the establishment.

They passed through a series of rooms, each dedicated to different games of chance. In one, men hunched over green baize tables, intent on their cards. In another, a roulette wheel spun, the ivory ball clicking against the wooden dividers. The walls were adorned with paintings of scantily clad women and scenes from Greek mythology, their gilt frames gleaming in the lamplight.

Wigton approached a corpulent man in an ill-fitting waistcoat who seemed to be overseeing the proceedings. "Mr. Fitch," he said, "might we have a word?"

Fitch eyed them suspiciously. "And who might you be?"

"Antony Wigton, solicitor. This is Mr. Reed Lydney. We're here about the late Lord Harlow."

Fitch's expression softened slightly. "Ah, poor Denis. Come to my office, gentlemen."

He led them to a small room off the main gambling floor. It was sparsely furnished with a desk, a few chairs, and a large safe in one corner. Fitch settled his bulk behind the desk and gestured for them to sit.

"What can I tell you about Lord Harlow?" he asked, pulling out a ledger.

Reed leaned forward. "We need to know about his debts, Mr. Fitch. How much did he owe, and to whom?"

Fitch pulled a book from his drawer and his fingers traced down a column of figures. "Lord Harlow was a frequent visitor, but he always settled his debts to the house promptly. His final plays were two days before his death. He lost heavily that night. Nearly two thousand pounds."

Reed felt his breath catch. It was more money than he had ever seen in one place.

"But," Fitch continued, "he paid it off the next day. Came in with a bank draft, looking pale as a ghost."

"Do you know if he borrowed money from anyone else?" Wigton asked. "Perhaps to cover his losses?"

Fitch shrugged. "Can't say for certain, but there was a gent who seemed to take an interest in Harlow. Foreign chap, Russian I think. Name of Litvinov."

Reed and Wigton exchanged a glance. "Did you ever see them speaking?" Reed asked.

"Once or twice," Fitch said. "Always very hushed conversations. Litvinov would sometimes watch Harlow play, but never joined the games himself."

"One more thing," Reed said. "Do you recognize the name Colin Sinclair?"

Fitch nodded. "An associate of Mr. Litvinov, if I'm not mistaken. I have seen him here several times but he prefers to watch the games rather than partake."

As they left the Gilded Serpent, Reed felt a mixture of relief and unease. They had confirmed Litvinov's connection to Denis, but the implications were troubling. The cool night air was a welcome respite from the stifling atmosphere inside, and Reed found himself taking deep breaths to clear his head.

"Well," Wigton said, "that was informative. What do you make of it?"

Reed shook his head. "I'm not sure, but I think we're only beginning to uncover the depth of Denis's troubles. And this Litvinov character... I fear he may be at the heart of it all."

Chapter 20
Binney Street
Israel

Israel used one of the tuppence Reed had given him for the omnibus to Fleet Street, but walked the rest of the way back to Hackney.

"We thought that Lydney had kidnapped you," Silas said as he walked in the door. "I saw the way he looked at you in the office. Like you were a delicious plum pudding and he hadn't eaten for weeks."

Israel's face reddened. "He is gentleman, and I am who I am. No pudding."

"I wouldn't be sure," Silas said, and laughed. "He said you had already met before. Was that at the brothel where you worked?"

"Man like Reed would not go to such a place," Israel said indignantly. He took a deep breath. "He see me when I am handing out flyers. One of them blow away and he catch it. He bring it to me. Then we have tea together."

Silas guffawed. "That's what you call it now?"

Israel was sure that he was as red as a tomato. "Tea house. We drink tea and talk. That is all."

"Stop tormenting the poor man, Silas," Ezra said. "We thought you would not have eaten so we saved you some dinner."

"Thank you," Israel said. He hadn't realized how hungry he was until Ezra placed a bowl of aromatic stew in front of him.

"*Adafina*," Ezra said. "A Sephardic stew my mother used to make. With meat, chickpeas, potatoes, and eggs."

"It smell delicious," Israel said. He tried a spoonful. "Thank you, Ezra. You and Silas so kind to me."

"We must look after each other," Ezra said.

Israel thought about that phrase as he prepared for bed that night. He and Ezra shared a Jewish faith, and all three of them were bound by their desires for the company of men. He realized that he felt more comfortable with them than he ever had in shul, or in his studies with Rabbi Adler. Here he could be fully who he was.

That reminded him of Reed Lydney. How did Reed feel, tied in by the constraints of his society? Could he be who he was? And did he want to be with Israel?

The next morning he reversed his journey from the night before. He walked to Fleet Street, and then used the second tuppence Reed had given him to take the omnibus to Bloomsbury Square. Reed answered his knock and smiled. "So glad it's you," he said. "And not another of those pestilent bill-collectors. I have already had one this morning, who I put off with promises. We must get a handle on income today."

"I am here to work," Israel said.

Reed took Israel's overcoat and they walked together to Denis's office. Despite all the work they had done the day before, there were still piles of papers and folders to go through.

They worked tirelessly throughout the day, the hours slipping by unnoticed. It wasn't until Israel's stomach growled loudly that he realized it must be time for lunch.

Reed heard it, and laughed. "I must not work you too hard," he said. "Come, let us see what Mrs. Clarkson can rustle up for luncheon."

"Your sister... she join us?"

"I have set her a task of her own," Reed said as they walked to the dining room. "Cataloging and responding to notes of condolence. Antony Wigton has volunteered to help her organize the correspondence. She has been working in her bedroom this morning, and he will arrive this afternoon to help."

Reed stuck his head through the kitchen door. "Is there any possibility of luncheon?" he asked.

"Of course," Israel heard Mrs. Clarkson say. "I have shepherd's pie with Brussels sprouts almost ready. Joe, run up and fetch Lady Harlow, if you will."

The boy hurried past them up the stairs, and Reed and Israel sat. "Is most generous of you to provide me with meal," Israel said.

"Nonsense. You are working in our house. We must take care of you."

"That is how I feel with Ezra and Silas," Israel said. "They take care of me. I do not know how I am so fortunate."

"I would say that God has recognized your affliction and your goodness, and provided for you. Would you not agree?"

"My relationship with God difficult now," Israel said. "I must believe in him, but I must separate what I was taught in yeshiva with what I know in my heart."

"Believing in your heart is always a good choice," Reed said, and his smile sent a feeling of warmth through Israel.

Then Cadence joined them, full of chatter about how dreadful some of the condolence cards had been. "It is truly not necessary of them to refer to the manner of Denis's death," she said. "I find that in poor taste. Enough simply to express their sadness."

"I agree," Reed said, as Mrs. Clarkson brought out the food. They ate, and talked, and Reed and Israel told Cadence what they had discovered.

Israel was surprised at how easy it was to talk to Cadence. She was so beautiful, and a lady as well, and yet she had the same charm and good humor as her brother.

"Do you know anything of an address on Binney Street in Mayfair?" Reed asked.

Cadence shook her head. "Should I?"

"Denis apparently owned a piece of property there. We found a deed in his papers but no other records of it. It doesn't appear to be leased out to anyone."

"That's very curious."

"I think Israel and I will go over there after luncheon and see what we can find."

"Remember, Antony Wigton is arriving this afternoon," Cadence said. "It would not be proper for the two of us to be alone in the house."

"We will make it a quick trip," Reed said. After slices of seed cake, he sent Israel to the office to search among Denis's keys for one that might open the door at the house on Binney Street.

As Mrs. Clarkson cleared the table, she looked down the hall to the office. "That young man," she said quietly to Cadence, "with those soulful dark eyes of his - he's likely to break a few hearts before he's done." She shook her head with a motherly smile. "Though he seems far too gentle a soul to do it on purpose."

Reed smiled, happy that someone else found Israel as attractive as he did.

When he joined Israel in the search for keys, they came up with several choices. Reed placed them in the pocket of his greatcoat, and they left the house and stepped out into the bustling London streets.

The early afternoon sun was welcome after so many days of fog and gray air. It illuminated the crowded thoroughfares, as they dodged horse-drawn carriages and street vendors hawking their wares. The walk wasn't particularly long, but the press of the crowd and the uneven cobblestones made their progress slow.

They arrived at a very simple house of red brick, with white-framed windows. Only two stories, it sat quietly between more impressive neighbors whose imposing façades were a testament to wealth and status. Reed rapped smartly on the door. Silence. He tried again, the sound echoing in the quiet street. Still nothing.

The curtains were drawn and the house appeared unoccupied.

The stoop was dusty but the brass doorknob was worn. Reed tried the first three keys without luck, but the fourth one opened the door.

The hallway smelled of tobacco and must. To the right was a large room without a bit of furniture, but the room on the right held a large round table and eight spindle-backed chairs.

"Curious," Reed said. They walked through to the kitchen at the rear, which was very simple. A bin held an empty spirit flask, a broken pewter tankard, and wrappers from fish and chips. Israel wrinkled his nose.

"No one has been here for a while," Reed said. "At least not since Denis's death."

"What we do?" Israel asked.

"We should haul out this trash," Reed said. "And explore the upstairs."

Israel gathered the empty bottles and wrappers into the bin.

"We should have these properly collected," Reed said. "We will have to discover when the rubbish men come through this area. But leave it for now. Let's explore the upstairs."

Reed climbed to the second floor. There were two rooms up there, both empty. "No beds," Israel said. "So no mistress."

"I agree. I don't see Denis doing the blanket hornpipe on that table downstairs."

Israel looked at him curiously, and Reed's face reddened. "Sorry. I meant, well, you know, sex."

"Sex on table," Israel said. He felt his cock stiffening at the thought of Reed, his clothes pulled apart, sitting on that table with his cock ready to be sucked.

Reed must have noticed, because his trousers swelled as well. Israel decided to be daring. "You have... on table?"

Reed would not look at him. "In Madeira, once. At a tavern." He looked up directly at Israel. "With another sailor."

Israel's mouth dropped open. So it was true! Reed enjoyed the company of other men—at least he had while he was a sailor.

He had been so lonesome for so long. He could not resist. He reached over and placed his hand on Reed's trouser front, feeling the stiffness beneath.

Reed's dropped jaw matched Israel's own. Something primal took over then, an impulse he could not control. He dropped to his knees and pushed Reed gently back against the wall. Then carefully he undid Reed's flies so that his trousers fell open. His excitement had already wetted the front of his undershorts, and Israel carefully peeled them down to expose his cock.

Reed shivered as Israel gripped his thighs. Then he leaned in and lightly licked Reed's cock, from the root to the tip. Reed moaned lightly and put his hand on Israel's head.

Israel had little experience, but what he had returned to him. He licked and sucked as Reed shook beneath him and emitted small cries of pleasure. "Oh, oh," Reed said. "Oh, Israel."

Israel did not respond except by licking and sucking more enthusiastically, until Reed could hold back no longer, and he spent in Israel's mouth. Israel swallowed it all and then sat back on the floor. "Was good?" he asked with a smile.

"It was very good," Reed said. He reached down and lifted Israel from the floor. "You are so skinny. We must fatten you up more."

"Is what Ezra says."

"But you don't.... with Ezra?"

Israel laughed. "Oh, I think Silas will cut off my cock if I try."

"We can't have that," Reed said. He pulled Israel into an embrace, and their mouths found each other. Israel's heart raced at the intimacy of it. Reed kissing him deeply even after what they had just done, tasting himself on Israel's lips and tongue. The kiss was tender yet hungry, as if Reed wanted to devour every trace of their shared pleasure.

Israel melted against him, overwhelmed by the way Reed held him, touched him, claimed him. It was so different from the furtive encounters of his past. This was a kiss that spoke of caring, of desire that went beyond the physical, and Israel found himself trembling with the intensity of his feelings.

The Lord's Gambit

Eventually Reed pulled back, though Israel could have stayed in that hallway kissing him for hours. "Now it is time for me to return the favor."

He tied up his flies.

"Is not necessary," Israel said, though his cock pulsed at the thought of Reed's lips on it.

"On the contrary, it is quite necessary," Reed said. "A gentleman always pays his debts. I believe you said something about a table?"

Israel's face reddened as he realized what Reed meant. Reed began down the stairs, his step jaunty. "Come along now. I intend to take my time with you."

Israel hurried behind him, almost stumbling on the stairs. They walked into the dining room and Reed motioned to the table. "Trousers off, and up you go."

Israel stood there stunned for a moment, then hurriedly undid his trousers and pulled them and his undershorts down. Reed motioned with a finger to the table.

Keeping his eyes on Reed, Israel moved backward, then hoisted himself up. He felt so wanton, so exposed, his trousers and shorts at his ankles, his cock standing up like a slightly tilted flagpole. "I have never tasted a Hebrew before," Reed said. He licked his lips. I am eager to try."

And then Reed dropped to his knees on the threadbare carpet and took Israel into his mouth. Israel gasped at the warm wetness enveloping him, his hands gripping the edge of the table where the polished wood pressed against his bare skin.

He felt exposed, vulnerable, yet completely safe under Reed's tender ministrations. Reed's hands held his bony hips with such gentleness, thumbs stroking small circles on his skin, as his blond head bobbed up and down. The sight of this beautiful, refined man on his knees, pleasuring him with such obvious desire and care, made Israel's heart race as much as his body's rising need.

It had been so long since anyone had touched him with such reverence, if indeed anyone ever had. Already overwhelmed from the intimacy of pleasuring Reed, Israel felt himself climbing rapidly toward his peak. He moaned helplessly, his thighs trembling under Reed's hands, his whole body shaking with the intensity of sensation and emotion combined.

When he finally spent, it was with a cry that seemed to come from his very soul, pleasure washing through him in waves as Reed continued to caress him with lips and tongue until the very end.

Reed sat back on his haunches, smiling as he licked his lips. "You know I have wanted to do that since we sat across from each other at that tea shop," he said.

"Was worth waiting for?" Israel said, as he slid down from the table.

Reed stood up. "Most certainly," he said, and he kissed Israel again. "And now, we need to return to Bloomsbury Square to chaperon my sister."

Chapter 21
Travel Arrangements
Reed

Reed's brain raced as they walked back to Bloomsbury Square. His heart bubbled with delight at the thought of a very special friendship with Israel Kupersmit. It would have to be a secret from Cadence, however. A secret from everyone. Could they find a reason to keep returning to Binney Street? But he knew they'd want a bed eventually.

That reminded him that he needed to travel to Gloucestershire to research the assets there. Of course, Israel would have to accompany him.

"Why you think Denis keep that house?" Israel asked.

"I have no idea." He looked at Israel and smiled. "But I'm glad he did."

"Silas can research ownership," Israel said. "He knows to do such things."

"Excellent idea. And you will have to accompany me to the family estate in Gloucestershire. I'm sure we will find more information there on assets and debts."

Reed watched Israel's face, wondering if he was concerned about visiting an English country house. Would the servants treat him poorly because he was Jewish? But surely his mathematical skills and quick mind would prove his worth. And more selfishly, Reed thrilled at the thought of having Israel to himself, away from London's prying eyes. Perhaps they could find private moments together, like they had in the house on Binney Street.

"How we get there?" Israel asked, his voice carefully neutral.

Reed pondered for a moment. "We'll take the train," he replied. "I'll make the arrangements. We should leave tomorrow morning."

They walked back to the house, the streets now bathed in the golden light of a clear afternoon. Reed and Israel returned to Denis's office, where they had already made significant progress on establishing what Denis had inherited from his father, and what he had sold. There were some shares in a fund still remaining. The house in Bloomsbury Square, the house on Binney Street, and the properties in Gloucestershire—to be evaluated in person.

Once they had returned to Denis's office, Reed's heart quickened at the thought of traveling with Israel. They would have to take rooms at an inn, or perhaps stay at Drayton House itself. He imagined lying beside Israel in a grand four-poster bed, no need to part at dawn, time to explore each other's bodies slowly instead of the rushed encounter they'd shared at Binney Street.

Would Israel be shy about undressing fully? Would he let Reed kiss every inch of his skin, show him how precious he was?

Reed heard the knock at the front door and glanced at the clock on the mantel. Three o'clock precisely. Wigton was nothing if not punctual. He walked out to the salon, where he waited as Mrs. Clarkson ushered Wigton in. He cut a dashing figure in his well-tailored coat, his hat tucked neatly under one arm.

Cadence appeared at the top of the stairs, a vision in black crepe that couldn't quite dim her natural beauty. Reed noticed the way Wigton's eyes widened almost imperceptibly, the slight catch in his breath as Cadence descended. For her part, Cadence's cheeks colored faintly, her eyes downcast as she greeted their guest.

"Mr. Wigton, how kind of you to come," she said softly.

The Lord's Gambit

"The pleasure is all mine, Lady Harlow," Wigton replied, his voice warm.

"We appreciate your continued help," Reed said. "Your guidance on these responses has been invaluable."

"It remains my pleasure," Wigton said. "I know from my housemate's recent loss how overwhelming these duties can be."

Wigton offered his arm to Cadence, and they walked into the salon. As was proper, the door remained open. He saw them sit at a small table, piles of cards between them.

Through the open door, Reed glimpsed Wigton helping Cadence sort condolence letters. When Wigton showed her how to properly seal an envelope, their fingers touched, lingering longer than propriety dictated.

Israel noticed Reed watching them and whispered, "They find comfort in each other, yes?" Reed nodded, seeing how Wigton's eyes softened when Cadence smiled, how she seemed to glow in his presence despite her mourning clothes.

The afternoon wore on, punctuated by the scratch of pens and the rustle of papers. Every so often, a burst of laughter would drift from the salon, causing Reed to look up sharply. He caught Israel's eye, raising an eyebrow.

"They sound like having good time," Israel observed, his English imperfect but his perception keen.

Reed nodded, a small frown creasing his brow. "Indeed they do," he murmured. "Well, I will begin on our travel arrangements."

He had never been to Denis's country estate, but Cadence had gone with him once, and they had gone by train from Paddington Station to Gloucester, and then a carriage to the estate in Little Witcombe. "At what time tomorrow would you be available?"

"Whatever suit you," Israel said.

"There is a railway ticket office in Mayfair, not far from here. I'll walk over and make our arrangements. Shouldn't be too long."

"I continue organizing documents," Israel said.

Reed checked his pockets for ready cash. In gold, he had three sovereigns and five half-sovereigns, as well as a handful of silver. That would get them to Gloucester and pay for a carriage to Little Witcombe. He had no idea what they would do for food; as far as he knew the house was closed and the staff dismissed.

He got up and walked into the salon, where he surprised Cadence and Wigton with their heads together. Cadence looked up quickly and her face colored. "Sorry to bother you, sister, but Israel and I are going to Little Witcombe tomorrow. Will there be carriages at the station in Gloucester? And is there a pub in town where we could stay and eat?"

"Yes, I recall there were several carriages for hire at the station," she said. "We stayed at the house and ate there, but I understand there is a pub in town. If you don't mind living without staff you could stay at the manor. The beds are quite comfortable though the house will be stuffy after being closed all this time."

He thanked her and returned to Israel. "I'm going out to the ticket office," he said. "I hesitate to ask, but would you mind if we traveled second-class rather than first? I do need to economize where we can."

"I travel third-class when I come here from boat in Southampton," he said. "Is fine for me."

"Perhaps for you alone, but you will be with me, and I require at least second-class comfort." Then he lowered his voice. "You will keep an ear out for the salon? You understand it is awkward to have Cadence and Wigton alone together."

"Is same when Jewish boy and girl are together," Israel said. "I listen."

Reed donned his greatcoat, scarf and hat and walked outside. The sun had disappeared, replaced by a cold March wind that whipped around the corner of Great Russell Street, carrying the sharp scent of coal smoke and rain-washed stone. The sidewalks were thick with men and women hurrying about their business, black coats and bowler hats moving like a river of ink through the gray afternoon.

He passed a flower seller with early spring daffodils, their yellow heads bobbing in the morning air, which made him wonder what Little Witcombe and Drayton House would be like. Would flowers welcome them? Or would the house and grounds be in disarray?

At the ticket office the brass grille between him and the clerk gleamed dully in the gray light that filtered through the sooty windows. He requested two round-trip second-class tickets to Gloucester for the next morning at ten, leaving the return open. The trip would take about two hours, putting them in town in time for lunch at the pub.

He watched as the elderly clerk adjusted his wire-rimmed spectacles and consulted a massive leather-bound timetable. Then Reed counted out the sovereigns onto the worn mahogany counter while the clerk's steel nib scratched across the heavy card stock.

When he returned to Bloomsbury Square, close to five o'clock, he looked in at the salon. Cadence and Wigton had their heads bent close together as they examined a sheet of paper. There was an ease between them, a shared secret in their smiles.

Reed cleared his throat, causing them both to start slightly.

The two separated quickly, and Reed noted the heightened color in Cadence's face. "Mr. Wigton has been most helpful," Cadence said. "I had no idea there were so many nuances to responding to condolence letters."

Wigton inclined his head modestly. "Lady Harlow is a quick study. I'm sure she'll be navigating London society with ease in no time."

"Thank you for your assistance, Wigton," Reed said, perhaps a touch more brusquely than necessary. "I'm sure my sister appreciates your expertise."

"Oh, yes," Cadence said quickly. "Perhaps... perhaps we could continue tomorrow? There's still so much to learn."

Wigton's face brightened. "I would be delighted. Same time tomorrow, then?"

Reed noticed how Wigton leaned forward eagerly, his eyes never leaving Cadence's face. His sister's cheeks colored prettily as she met his gaze. Something passed between them, a shared understanding that transcended words. Wigton's fingers tapped nervously on his knee, and Cadence smoothed her skirts with unusual attention, both clearly aware of each other in a way that went beyond mere social courtesy.

"There is a problem," Reed said. "Israel and I must leave tomorrow morning for Gloucestershire to investigate the situation at the estate. It would not be proper for you and Mr. Wigton to be unchaperoned."

Wigton's face clouded. "Of course."

"What about Mrs. Clarkson?" Cadence asked. "She'll be here in the house."

"In the kitchen," Reed said.

"Then we can work in there," Cadence said.

Reed looked from Wigton to his sister. "I suppose that would be all right. As long as Mrs. Clarkson agrees."

Cadence's smile grew. "I'm sure she will. Thank you, Reed."

As Reed saw Wigton to the door, he couldn't help but notice the spring in his old school friend's step, the lingering glance he cast back towards the stairs where Cadence stood.

Closing the door, Reed turned to find Israel watching him, a knowing look in his dark eyes.

"What you think about your sister and Mr. Wigton?" Israel asked quietly.

Reed sighed, running a hand through his hair. "I think, my friend, that I must keep an eye on the situation. Cadence is still in mourning, after all."

But as he spoke, Reed couldn't quite shake the feeling that, mourning or not, something had shifted that afternoon. Something that might prove as complex and intriguing as the mystery they were trying to unravel.

Chapter 22
A Meaningless Act
Israel

Before Israel left Bloomsbury Square, Reed insisted that Israel take two more coins to cover his travel home and to the station the next morning. He accepted them, and repeated what he had done the night before.

As he rode atop the omnibus, he felt a touch of spring in the air. But maybe it was simply the memory of what he and Reed had done that afternoon. It was so different from the last time he had been with a man.

He had always thought of his desire for men as a curse, a thing to be hidden away in dark alleys and behind taverns. But Reed made it feel like a blessing. The way Reed's eyes softened when their gazes met, the gentle press of his lips, the careful way he held Israel as if he were something precious. It transformed what had been furtive and shameful into something approaching holy.

Even the act itself felt sanctified by Reed's tenderness. Each movement was a question, each touch asked permission. Israel had never felt so seen, so cherished. His body responded not just with desire but with a deeper yearning: to be known, to be loved, to be accepted completely.

The omnibus swayed as it rolled over the cobblestones, and as

Israel closed his eyes his body still hummed from the afternoon with Reed. It had been gentle, careful. So different from that other time, only a few months before, the encounter that had changed everything.

Rabbi Adler had dismissed the students early that Friday afternoon, so they could get home and prepare for Shabbos. But since Israel was only a boarder in the teacher's house, he had no reason to rush. As he made his way back, he stopped behind a tavern, where the oven inside sent out gusts of warm air into the alley.

A horse-drawn dray pulled into the alley, blocking Israel's way out. A strapping delivery man only a few years older than he was hopped down and set up a plank from the back of the wagon to the cobblestones. "Here, give us a hand, will you?" he asked Israel. "There's a sixpence in it for your trouble."

Israel was always eager to earn a bit of pocket change, so he helped the man roll the hogsheads off the cart and into the back of the tavern. The man had reddish brown hair and despite the cold his sleeves were rolled up to his elbows, revealing a trace of brown hair there as well. The bunching up of the sleeve accented the musculature of his upper arms.

As he worked, Israel kept stealing glances at the man. His strong calves, his tight buttocks—and the cock that pushed against the front of his trousers, long and hard. His mouth watered.

They finished the job and the man reached into his trouser pocket, stretching the fabric taut against the hardness of his cock. He watched Israel's eyes and smiled. Then he pulled out the sixpence and tossed it to Israel, who caught it in the air.

"And how about a tip?" the man asked. He stared directly at Israel and without looking down, opened his flies and released his cock. Israel had seen other boys naked while bathing, but never a non-Jewish man.

He was stunned to see a layer of flesh over the tip. He realized suddenly that this was what marked Jews from other men, that the flesh had been cut away from his cock at eight days old.

Without consciously thinking, he crossed to the man, then went down on knees on the damp cobblestones. He opened his mouth and the man aimed his cock toward him. He knew from his own experience that his cock reacted to being pulled on, so he tried that with his mouth.

"Watch them teeth!" the man said.

Israel moved up and down on the man's cock, figuring it out as he went. He licked, he sucked. The man's body shivered, and he made a small sound. Then there was a heavy fluid spurting into Israel's mouth, and he backed off, choking.

"Israel?"

He looked at the far end of the alley. Rabbi Adler himself stood there. He couldn't move, and remained still as stone as the delivery man hopped onto the wagon, shook the reins, and took off.

There was no denying what Rabbi Adler had seen. A quick, meaningless act that had sent Israel careening down a terrible slope. Within a week, his whole life was over.

The memory of that brutal encounter behind the tavern made Israel shiver, but being in Reed's arms was something entirely different. Each touch spoke of reverence, of care. When Reed's fingers traced the curve of his jaw, Israel felt tears prick his eyes. Not from shame or fear, but from the sheer tenderness of it.

The omnibus turned a corner, and Israel shifted in his seat, pushing the memory away. That had been lust, nothing more. What he felt for Reed was different. Dangerous in its own way, perhaps, but different. Still, the old fear lingered. He touched his throat where Reed had kissed him, and wondered if he would ever truly be free of the past.

He was home early enough to dine with Ezra and Silas. He pushed open the familiar door, the scent of Ezra's cooking wrapping around him like an embrace. The small dining room was already warm from the fire, and both Ezra and Silas looked up from their conversation as he entered.

"Ah, our wandering scholar returns," Ezra said, rising to fetch another bowl. "And just in time for couscous with lamb and vegetables. Though perhaps you have grown too fine for such simple fare, now that you spend your days in Bloomsbury Square?"

"Not at all," Israel said. "Your cooking has taste of home."

Silas smiled, reaching for the wine. "And what discoveries did you make today?"

"Denis had secret property." He handed Silas a piece of paper with the address on Binney Street. "Tomorrow, you can find how he owns it, please?"

Silas took the paper. "Binney Street. That's near Bloomsbury Square, isn't it? Secret sex den for the lord?"

Israel felt his face coloring as he recalled what he and Reed had done in that house. "No, no beds," he said. "Only one big table and chairs in dining room."

He saw Ezra and Silas share a glance and was afraid they had discovered his secret. "I can go to the Middlesex Land Registry Office," Silas said. "You didn't find any deeds in Lord Harlow's office?"

Irael shook his head.

"Well, you can come with me to the registry office," Silas said. "Something else for you to learn."

Israel shook his head. "Tomorrow morning Reed and I take train to Gloucester."

"You're going with him?" Silas asked. "Why?"

Israel shrugged. "He ask."

Once again, Silas and Ezra shared a look. Israel sniffed the air. Did he smell like sex? Was he giving away anything about what they had done? Surely Silas and Ezra would disapprove, because of the gulf between his station and Reed's.

"The countryside is a dangerous place," Ezra warned, his wooden spoon pointing at Israel for emphasis. "Full of ignorant people who have never seen a Jew before. You must be careful."

"Speak as little as possible," Silas said. "Make sure to shave your beard carefully. You don't want anyone to notice you are a foreigner. At least the new clothes Ezra bought will help you pass."

He took a sip of wine, then added, "Speaking of answers, I made some progress today. I visited three of the moneylenders Lord Harlow owed. Two of them mentioned the name of Colin Sinclair. Apparently, he was asking questions about his lordship's debts just last week."

Israel leaned forward. "Name on paper you found. Who is this Sinclair?"

"That's what I spent the afternoon discovering. He's a solicitor with offices near Lincoln's Inn Fields. More interesting still, one of the firm's clients is Sergei Litvinov."

The couscous suddenly tasted like sand in Israel's mouth. "Litvinov," he repeated. "Russian moneylender Lord Harlow owed?"

"The very same," Silas confirmed. "Though why Sinclair's solicitor would be investigating his lordship's debts after his death... that's a question worth pondering, wouldn't you say?"

Ezra shook his head. "Politics and money make a dangerous combination. You take care in Gloucester, Israel. Something about this business feels wrong."

"I am careful," Israel promised, but his mind was already racing ahead to tomorrow's journey. What would they find at the estate? And what did Litvinov want with Denis's debts?

The conversation turned to other matters, including Ezra's plans for Passover, and an article Silas had read about Britain's relations with Russia. But Israel found himself only half-listening. The mystery of Denis's death seemed to grow more complex with each passing day, and now he and Reed were heading into unknown territory.

Chapter 23
Great Western Railway
Reed

At dinner that evening, Reed told Mrs. Clarkson that he and Israel were traveling the next day, and asked if she could pack them provisions. "I think we will need to rough it at the house for a meal or two."

"I can easily prepare you some cold roast chicken and potatoes," she said.

When she returned to the kitchen, Cadence turned to Reed. "Are you sure this is a wise adventure, brother? Perhaps the clerk, Silas, could go to Drayton House. Or Mr. Wigton. I could even accompany him, as I have been there before."

"You know very well you could not travel to Gloucester with Mr. Wigton without a chaperone," Reed said. "And remember, you are in mourning. Surely Mr. Wigton informed you of the conditions."

Cadence frowned. "He brought black-bordered stationery with him the first time he arrived, which is all I may use for correspondence. For deep mourning, which could last a year, I must wear all black clothing, including mourning crepe, and a widow's cap and veil when in public. Mr. Wigton helped me look through the cabinets upstairs in search of a suitable one. Fortunately I found one of those that had belonged to some awful relative of Denis's when I went through the cabinets."

"You and Mr. Wigton went upstairs together?"

"There was nothing untoward between us," Cadence insisted. "And Mrs. Clarkson was in the kitchen directly below us."

"You must not tell anyone else about that," Reed said. "Seriously, Cadence. You could be cast out of society."

"And what has society done for me?" she demanded. "Except put me under so many rules and regulations that sometimes I feel my back would break from the burdens?"

Her eyes flashed. "When we were first married, Denis constantly lectured me about how I was to behave. I did my best to be a proper, demure wife. We hardly went out together, because he complained that I might embarrass him with my country manners. Now I realize that he was ignoring me in favor of those gambling hells. And probably whores!"

"We have found no evidence of whores," Reed said gently. "And I believe that if he ignored you, it wasn't due to embarrassment. You know that his father pressured him to marry and that Denis found you a beautiful candidate."

"Beautiful and acceptable," she said. "To father and son. I was not worldly-wise enough to recognize my predicament." She frowned. "And now it is no better. I am not to wear any jewelry except jet. Not even the pearls Denis gave to me on our wedding. No social events or entertainment and only minimal social calls. I am as much a prisoner now as I was when he was alive."

"But at least now you can see a way forward," Reed said. "You are young and beautiful and eventually we will establish your income. After your period of mourning ends, you may begin to cultivate friends, and perhaps even gentlemen callers."

"That is still two years from now," Cadence said, and she began to cry. "What am I to do between now and then? Even when I can begin to go out, how do I start? Perhaps I shall retire to Drayton House and live out my life with cows and sheep."

Reed burst into laughter. "I can hardly see you as a shepherdess," he said. "No, my dear, you were meant for a social life in London. And if Mr. Wigton has patience, he may become your guide, when it is appropriate."

She dried her eyes with her napkin. "Do you think so?"

He reached across the table and took her hand. "I am sure of it."

That night, as he took off his trousers, the smell of sex rose. Slight, almost covered by the perfumed soap Cadence kept in the cabinets. He brought his shorts to his nose and inhaled, remembering Israel and what they had done.

There were beds in Drayton House, Cadence had said. No staff. So he and Israel could get up to all kinds of mischief, if they chose, without having to hide.

As he washed and then donned his nightshirt, he realized he had never spent the night in the same bed as another man after coitus. There had been times commuting to School when he had shared beds with other boys in tavern accommodations, but nothing had ever come of it. And when he was in the Navy, his assignations had been brief and without passion.

How different was his time with Israel! Though it was quick, it was suffused with a desire such as he had not known before. Each touch of Israel's lips on his cock, each caress of his thighs from Israel's smooth hands. Those were the hands of a scholar, a lover of books, a man Reed might be able to share his heart with.

The dark intensity of Israel's eyes had captivated him from their first meeting - pools of amber flecked with intelligence and sensitivity that seemed to draw light into them. Even gaunt from his recent hardships, Israel moved with an inherent grace, his high cheekbones casting elegant shadows, his full lips curving into shy smiles that made Reed's heart race.

His dark curls had a slight wave that softened his angular features, and when he spoke of poetry or numbers, his entire face lit up with passion. Reed found himself entranced not just by Israel's physical beauty, but by the quiet strength and dignity that radiated from within.

He went to sleep in a shaft of moonlight, thinking of the days to come.

The next morning dawned cold but clear. Reed ate a hurried breakfast served by Mrs. Clarkson, and then Israel arrived and they set out for the station. The streets were already busy with early morning traffic. Delivery wagons bringing bread and milk, clerks walking briskly to their offices, maids beating carpets in front gardens.

The cavernous train shed of Paddington Station bustled with activity as Reed and Israel made their way through the morning crowd. The station's wrought-iron and glass roof arched high above them, its intricate design filtering the weak March sunlight. The air was thick with a mixture of coal smoke, steam, and the musty scent of damp wool coats.

Porters in uniform scurried about, pushing trolleys laden with trunks and valises. The clatter of their wheels on the stone floor mingled with the hiss of steam engines and the shrill whistle of trains preparing to depart. Everywhere, the rhythmic clack-clack of boots and shoes on the platform added to the station's lively symphony.

Gentlemen in top hats and frock coats strode purposefully towards their trains, while ladies in practical walking dresses with modest bustles and sturdy bonnets gathered in small groups, saying their goodbyes. A newsboy's shout cut through the din as he waved the morning papers, headlines trumpeting the latest news from Parliament and the continent.

Reed checked his pocket watch, its golden case gleaming in the gaslight. "Our train leaves in fifteen minutes," he said to Israel. "Platform three."

They made their way to the second-class carriages, their polished wooden sides a deep, rich brown. A guard in a smart uniform stood by the open door, checking tickets and assisting passengers. The air grew warmer as they approached the waiting engine, its great iron form exuding heat and the promise of imminent departure.

Israel glanced around, taking in the organized chaos of the station. "Is always this busy?" he asked, his voice barely audible above the station's clamor.

Reed nodded, guiding them towards their carriage. "Welcome to the heart of London's railways, my friend. Paddington never sleeps."

As they boarded, the wooden benches of the second-class compartment offered a respite from the frenetic energy outside. The door closed behind them with a solid thunk, muffling the station's noise. Through the window, they watched as last-minute passengers hurried along the platform, and porters loaded the final pieces of luggage.

With a long, low whistle and a great exhalation of steam, the engine came to life. The carriage jerked gently, and they were off, leaving the ordered mayhem of Paddington behind as they set out for the mysteries that awaited them in Gloucestershire.

The carriage rattled westward, the compartment lit by the wan March light filtering through windows grimy with soot. Reed pressed his handkerchief to his nose as the locomotive's smoke occasionally gusted past their window. Israel seemed more entranced by the view outside the window than the railway's inevitable discomforts.

"We'll be passing through Reading shortly," Reed noted, consulting his pocket watch. "The Great Western's pride, this line. Brunel's work, though they've been converting the broad gauge these past few years."

The Thames Valley spread before them, fields beginning to show the first green haze of spring wheat, dotted with yellow clusters of early daffodils. The hedgerows were studded with bursting buds, and beneath the still-bare elms, patches of snowdrops and crocuses brightened the winter-brown earth.

Market gardens and dairy farms dominated the landscape, supplying London's endless appetite. Villages appeared and vanished: Maidenhead, Twyford, Reading with its brick buildings and brewery chimneys.

"The soil changes after Reading," Reed observed, noting the subtleties of the terrain. "Better suited to grazing than crops. Though my father wasn't a farmer, Cadence and I grew up in the country, so it was imbued in us from childhood."

He was charmed by Israel's enthusiasm over the countryside. "Was Poland like this?" he asked.

"I never know much of country," Israel said. "Our village too close to city."

As they passed into Berkshire proper, the landscape began to roll more prominently, chalk downs rising to their north. Occasional quarries scarred the hillsides, feeding the endless construction in London. They passed Didcot, where a branch line split southward toward Oxford, then Swindon. Reed had read about that great railway works town, which had sprung up from almost nothing in the past thirty years.

The carriage swayed as they curved through the Stroud Valley, the Cotswold Hills now rising more dramatically. They ate some of the provisions Mrs. Clarkson had prepared as they watched sheep graze on the steep hillsides, moving like dots of cloud-shadow across the green-brown slopes. Ancient beech woods crowned the hills, their bare branches stark against the winter sky.

The train slowed as they approached Gloucester, the great spire of the cathedral visible through the haze. Factory chimneys competed with it, their smoke joining the locomotive's own cloud. The carriage wheels clattered as they entered the station's approach, past goods yards stacked with timber, coal, and wool bales waiting for transport.

The train's whistle shrieked as they drew into Gloucester station, the platform already busy with porters and passengers despite the winter afternoon's early darkness. The two men stepped down onto the platform, their boots clicking on the stones, ready to face whatever awaited them at Denis's family seat.

Chapter 24
Drayton House
Israel

Israel watched appreciatively as Reed approached a weathered man with a cloth watch cap and negotiated with him for the trip to Little Witcombe. They tossed their satchels inside and climbed in, and the driver shook his reins to move the horse forward.

The hired carriage rattled over the cobblestones of Gloucester's outskirts, its wooden wheels raising a clatter that made conversation difficult. The driver, by name Hawkins, had his horse move at a steady pace along the rutted road that led southeast toward Little Witcombe.

Israel sat beside Reed on the front-facing seat, their thighs occasionally touching as the carriage swayed. The leather cushions were cracked and worn, but still preferable to the wooden benches of second-class rail travel. And Israel relished the moments when his thigh brushed against Reed's. He looked at Reed and smiled, and received a smile in return.

Through the windows, Israel watched as the cathedral spire receded behind them, while ahead the Cotswold Hills rose, their limestone faces scarred by quarries. The March weather was temperamental, alternating between weak sunshine and scudding clouds that threatened rain. As they left the town behind, the road wound through a landscape of winter-brown fields divided by dry stone walls. Occasionally they passed a farmer breaking ground for spring planting, or sheep grazing on the emerging grass.

"The roads are better maintained than where I grew up," Reed said, as they bounced over a particularly deep rut. "Though that's not saying much."

After an hour, they began to climb into the hills. The horse's pace slowed as the grade increased, and Israel smelled the fresh-turned earth from nearby fields. A group of laborers paused in their work to watch the carriage pass, leaning on their spades and whispering among themselves.

"We're nearly there," Reed said, consulting a letter from the property manager. "The entrance to Drayton House should be just around this bend."

The carriage turned off the main road onto a drive lined with ancient beech trees, their budding branches forming a cathedral-like arch overhead. Years of neglect showed in the untrimmed verges and crumbling stone walls that marked the boundary of the estate. Patches of moss grew thick on the north-facing stones, and several sections had collapsed, allowing sheep to wander freely across the boundary.

They passed a small lake, its surface ruffled by the March wind, where reed beds had grown wild and untended. On its far bank stood a boathouse with a sagging roof and missing shutters. A pair of swans glided past, seemingly the only inhabitants.

The drive curved again, and Drayton House came into view. It was a handsome Georgian manor of honey-colored Cotswold stone, three stories high with a slate roof and tall chimneys. But like the grounds, the house showed signs of recent neglect. Ivy grew unchecked up one corner, several window shutters hung askew, and the gravel sweep before the front door was overgrown with weeds.

"We should stop at the manager's cottage first," Reed said to the driver. "It's just ahead, where that smoke is rising."

The cottage was a sturdy stone building with a vegetable garden and chicken coop, at the edge of the home farm. As their carriage approached, a stocky man in working clothes emerged from the barn. He had the weathered face of a farmer, though his bearing suggested education above his station.

"That must be Thompson," Reed said. "Denis's father hired him from a larger estate when their previous manager died. Cadence said he was very capable."

The carriage drew to a halt, and Thompson approached, wiping his hands on his coat. His expression was guarded but not unwelcoming.

"Mr. Lydney?" he asked, as Reed descended. "I received your letter about his lordship's passing. Though I must say, we weren't expecting anyone from London so soon."

"Mr. Thompson, a pleasure. This is Mr. Kupersmit, who is assisting me with the estate's accounts." Reed's voice carried just the right note of authority tempered with respect. "I trust you can help us understand the current state of affairs here at Drayton House?"

Thompson's eyes moved from Reed to Israel, taking in the latter's appearance with careful consideration. "I'll do what I can, sir. Though I must warn you, things have been... difficult these past months. His lordship had some unusual requests regarding the estate's income."

Above them, Drayton House loomed against the gray sky, its empty windows like vacant eyes watching their arrival. A crow launched itself from one of the chimneys, its harsh call echoing across the silent grounds. Israel shivered, though whether from the chill air or the sense of secrets about to be revealed, he couldn't say.

"How is her ladyship?" Thompson asked. "She was only here once, but she made quite the impression on my wife. Beautiful and kind, as she recalls."

"My sister is indeed both those things," Reed said. "I shall tell her that you asked about her."

Thompson led them up the worn stone steps to Drayton House's main entrance, fishing a large ring of keys from his pocket. The heavy oak door creaked open, revealing a marble-floored entrance hall where their footsteps echoed in the emptiness. A massive chandelier hung above, its crystals dulled by dust.

"Mind where you step in the east corridor," Thompson said, pointing to their right. "We've had water coming in around the chimney there. Put buckets down when it rains." He gestured to dark stains on the plaster ceiling. "Been trying to get up there to fix it, but his lordship... well, he wasn't much interested in repairs these past months."

The house had the damp, musty smell of a place too long closed. As they moved through the ground floor, Thompson pulled dust sheets off furniture to reveal good, solid pieces that had seen better days. The library's shelves sagged with leather-bound volumes, their spines cracked from temperature changes and humidity.

"This hurts my heart," Reed said. "To see books treated this way."

"When you have money, I am sure you will treat these books well," Israel said.

"The drawing room's still sound," Thompson said, opening another door. "Though we had to move some furniture away from that wall—more water damage." He pointed to a corner where wallpaper had begun to peel. "But the fireplace works well enough. My wife can send over some coal if you'd like to use it."

"Yes, that would be good," Reed said. "No reason to pay for an inn if we can stay here."

Israel noticed Reed paying particular attention to the furniture and paintings. Many places showed empty spots where paintings had once hung, their outlines visible on the faded wallpaper.

They climbed the main staircase, its carved banister still elegant despite needing polish. On the first floor, Thompson showed them a bedroom with faded wallpaper. "This one is the driest," he said, opening the doors to a southern view. "The north side gets awful damp in winter. Lost two mattresses to mold before we learned to keep the fires going up here."

The room was large, with high ceilings and tall windows that looked out over the unkempt gardens. It had a four-poster bed with faded hangings, a washstand, and a fireplace. The furniture was good quality but showed signs of wear—worn spots on chair seats, slight wobbles to table legs.

"Be best if you could share the bed," he said. "Easier on my Rebecca. I can have her bring up some fresh linens. And perhaps you'd like something to eat? She's a fair hand in the kitchen, though nothing fancy like you'd get in London." He must have understood something from Israel's appearance or name, so he looked at him. "Anything you can't eat?"

"Anything is good," Israel said. If there was pork, he simply wouldn't eat it.

"That would be most welcome," Reed said. "We've only had Mrs. Clarkson's packed lunch on the train. Something simple would be perfect."

"Rebecca's made a good beef stew today," Thompson said. "Could have that sent over with some bread. And there's a bit of cheese."

"Perfect," Reed said. He glanced at Israel, who nodded eagerly.

"The kitchen below stairs is still functioning," Thompson continued, leading them back to the ground level. "Though we've closed off the old servants' quarters—too much work to maintain them all. The roof's sound over the main part of the house, but the north wing..." He shook his head. "That'll need attention before long."

They passed a music room where a pianoforte stood silent under its dust sheet. "Lady Harlow played when she visited," Thompson said. "Lovely it was, too. Brightened the whole house up."

"Yes, my sister is quite talented," Reed said. "She has not played since.... Well, some time."

In the kitchen, they found signs of recent use—clean pots hanging on hooks, a kettle on the massive range. "I'll send Rebecca over with some tea things," Thompson said. "And the stew later. There's plenty of wood stacked by the range if you want to warm the place up."

Looking around the huge kitchen with its ancient cabinets and worn flagstone floor, Israel could imagine how it must have been in better days, filled with servants and the smell of cooking. Now it felt hollow, waiting.

"One more thing," Thompson said, his voice lowered though they were alone in the house. "You should know... his lordship had visitors sometimes. Late at night. Men I didn't know. They'd arrive in a carriage, spend hours in the library, then leave before dawn. I never spoke of it, but..." He looked uncomfortable. "Given what happened to his lordship, perhaps you should know."

Reed and Israel exchanged glances. "When was the last such visit?" Reed asked carefully.

"About a week before he died," Thompson said. "Three men that time. Foreign-sounding, one of them. They left with a bundle of papers." He shrugged. "Not my place to question his lordship's business, but it never seemed right to me."

"Thank you," Reed said. "You've been very helpful. We'll need to go through his lordship's papers in the library. And perhaps you could show us the estate books tomorrow?"

"Of course, sir. I'll have Rebecca bring those supplies directly. Will you be wanting breakfast in the morning as well?"

Reed nodded. "If it's not too much trouble. And Mr. Thompson... we appreciate your discretion in these matters."

After Thompson left, Reed and Israel stood in the kitchen's fading light. The range had retained some heat from Thompson's earlier fire, but the rest of the house was growing cold as evening approached.

"Well," Reed said softly. "It seems Denis had more secrets than we knew." He moved closer to Israel, their shoulders touching. "At least we'll have privacy here to discuss them."

Israel felt warmth spread through him that had nothing to do with the range. "Yes," he said. "Much to discuss. But first, maybe we light fires? Is getting cold."

Reed smiled. "Yes, let's make ourselves comfortable. We may be here for several days."

Chapter 25
Flying Trapeze
Reed

Reed found Denis's office easily enough—it was the only room in the house that showed signs of recent use. Unlike the library, with its regimented rows of leather-bound books, this room was a jumble of papers, ledgers, and mismatched furniture. A large desk dominated the space, positioned to catch the light from tall windows that looked out over the neglected gardens.

The March wind whistled through gaps in the window frames, causing the heavy damask curtains to shift and sway. Reed pulled his coat tighter and glanced at Israel, who had already begun sorting through papers on the desk.

"Come sit beside me," Reed said, pulling a second chair close. "We'll work through these systematically." The chairs creaked as they settled, their shoulders touching. The contact sent a warmth through Reed that helped counter the room's persistent chill.

A scratching sound from behind the wainscoting made them both start. "Rats," Reed said. "Not surprising, given the state of things." But he found himself leaning closer to Israel nonetheless.

The afternoon light was already beginning to fade as they worked through pile after pile of correspondence, bills, and notes. The damp smell of the house was stronger here, mingled with the musty odor of old paper and ink. Every so often, a gust of wind would set papers flying, and they would scramble to catch them.

"Look at this," Israel said suddenly, his voice dropping to a whisper. He held up several sheets of heavy paper, each bearing an elaborate letterhead with Cyrillic text alongside English. "Is from Litvinov."

Reed leaned in closer, his chest pressing against Israel's shoulder as he read. The papers were IOUs, each for substantial sums. "Two thousand pounds... three thousand... good God, another for five thousand." His breath caught. "The total must be near fifteen thousand pounds."

"Is very much money," Israel said. His hand trembled slightly as he held the papers.

"More than the estate can possibly raise quickly," Reed said. He was acutely aware of Israel's proximity—the elegant line of his throat as he leaned forward, the way his dark curls fell across his forehead in a carelessly perfect sweep. Even with his too-thin frame, there was something magnetic about him, from the fine-boned architecture of his face to the grace with which he moved.

The slight spicy scent of his soap mingled with something uniquely him, warm and intoxicating. Without thinking, Reed reached out and touched Israel's hand where it rested on the desk, his fingers drawn to the delicate strength of those long, beautiful fingers.

The sound of footsteps in the corridor made them jump apart just as Rebecca Thompson appeared in the doorway, her arms full of linens. She was a small woman with bright eyes and rosy cheeks from the cold outside.

"Oh!" she exclaimed, clearly startled to find them so close together. "I'm sorry, sirs. I brought fresh sheets and blankets. And the stew's nearly ready—I can bring it up in about half an hour, if that suits?"

Reed found himself stammering slightly. "Yes, thank you, Mrs. Thompson. That would be perfect. We'll eat in the kitchen, if that's convenient?"

She nodded, her eyes darting between them before she turned to go. "Firewood is dear this late in the winter, so I only lit a fire in the one bedroom. But there is a set of linens for a second room if you prefer. The house gets that cold at night, you see."

After she left, Reed and Israel sat in awkward silence for a moment, listening to her footsteps fade away. The wind chose that moment to gust particularly strongly, rattling the windows and making the curtains dance.

"We should finish here," Reed said finally. "But first..." He gathered the IOUs and tucked them carefully into his coat pocket. "These we keep close. I don't want Thompson or anyone else knowing about them just yet."

Israel nodded, but his eyes were on Reed's face. "Is dangerous game Denis was playing," he said softly.

"Yes," Reed agreed. "And I fear we're only beginning to understand how dangerous." He stood, offering his hand to help Israel up. Their fingers lingered together for a moment longer than necessary before they began to tidy the papers on the desk.

A rat scurried across the floor as they were finishing, disappearing behind a bookcase. Its bold appearance seemed an ill omen, reminding them that they were interlopers here, disturbing long-held secrets in this declining house. The wind's mournful whistle through the house only reinforced the feeling as they made their way to the kitchen, where warmth and food awaited them.

Mrs. Thompson brought them the stew, and showed them where the dishes and silverware were kept. "And now I've got to get himself his dinner," she said. "Shall I bring up breakfast in the morning?"

"That would be lovely," Reed said. "Is eight o'clock too early for you?"

She laughed. "I'll be up at first light feeding the chickens and milking the cow. Eight o'clock is the middle of the morning for me."

She left, and Reed took down bowls while Israel retrieved silverware. Then Reed dished out the stew, which smelled heavenly. It tasted delicious, too.

"Country food," Israel said. "Always better than city. Closer to land."

"I agree," Reed said. "And school food is generally awful, despite being in the country."

They sat at the kitchen table, steam rising from bowls of stew that Rebecca had left them. The range's warmth barely reached them, and Israel had dragged his chair closer to Reed's, ostensibly for warmth.

"Food was bad?" Israel asked.

"Terrible. We had this thing called 'strike'—a sort of pudding made from leftover bread crusts boiled with milk and raisins. The older boys said it got its name because we should go on strike rather than eat it." Reed laughed softly. "But that wasn't the worst. One morning at breakfast, I was eating my porridge and found a dead mouse in it."

Israel made a face. "What you do?"

"I was sitting next to my friend Tony Wigton—yes, the same one who's now helping Cadence. He saw me go pale and quickly switched our bowls when no one was looking. Then he stood up and made a great fuss about finding a mouse in his porridge. The master on duty was horrified, the kitchen staff were summoned... and no one ever knew it was actually my bowl."

"He was good friend."

"Yes, he was. His family was much wealthier than mine, so his voice was more important that morning than mine could ever have been."

Reed broke off some bread. "But I couldn't tell Cadence about that in my letters. She was only twelve, and I wanted her to think I was having grand adventures. Instead, I wrote about the cricket matches, the Latin verses we learned, the books in the library, the grand stone buildings, the chapel with its spire, how the older boys wore tall hats to church on Sundays."

He paused, his eyes distant. "Then at Christmas, when I finally came home, she took one look at me and burst into tears. Said I'd grown too thin. She'd saved all her pocket money and bought me a whole jar of barley sugar sweets." His voice softened. "That was Cadence all over—always trying to take care of me, even then."

The wind howled outside, making the windows rattle. Israel moved his chair even closer. "You miss her, when you are there?"

"Terribly. We'd never been apart before." Reed stared into the fire. "I was so frightened that first night at school. Not of the other boys or the masters, but that I would somehow become a different person, someone Cadence wouldn't recognize when I returned home."

"You fear losing yourself?" Israel asked softly. "I understand this. When I first come to London, I write letters home every day. Then less and less, as I change more and more."

"Did your family accept those changes?"

Israel's hand found Reed's in the firelight. "No. When they discover... when they learn what I am, letters stop. Is like door closing forever." He swallowed hard. "Sometimes I dream of knocking on that door again. But person they want me to be, he is ghost now."

"And the person you are?" Reed's thumb traced circles on Israel's palm.

"Is still becoming. Like butterfly emerging from cocoon. Scared, but also... hopeful." He looked at Reed. "Because now I have someone who sees me, real me."

"You have such courage," Reed whispered. "To remake yourself in truth rather than hide behind acceptable lies."

"You also have courage. To find way to be both gentleman and..." Israel gestured between them with their joined hands.

"Both. Yes. Perhaps that's what we're learning together. How to be both."

They sat in comfortable silence then, finishing their meal, while the wind continued its lonely song outside and the flames flickered in the range. "Must be like this for Ezra and Silas," Israel said. "When I am not there."

"There is another side to the coupling between two people,"

Reed said. "Companionship. Friendship. I never thought I would be able to enjoy that."

"Because you only want men?"

"Yes, and what I saw of Cadence and Denis. There was no ease between them. Have you ever been to a circus?"

Israel shook his head. "No circus in Poland. In London, is not allowed, when I study with rabbi."

Reed sighed. How to explain? "Well, they're quite remarkable. Astley's Amphitheatre in London pioneered them—a great round building with a ring in the center where horses gallop in circles while acrobats perform tricks on their backs. But the most breathtaking act happens high above."

He gestured upward toward the kitchen's oak-beamed ceiling. "They string ropes across the height of the building, maybe forty feet up. And there, suspended on swinging bars, the aerialists perform what they call the flying trapeze."

Israel's eyes widened. "They fly?"

"In a manner of speaking. Two performers swing out from platforms on opposite sides. They must time their movements perfectly—when to release their grip, when to reach out, when to grasp each other's hands. For a moment, they hang suspended in the air, connected only to each other."

Reed's voice softened. "That's what Cadence and Denis were like. Two people swinging past each other in the great social circus of London. Sometimes they would catch each other, make that perfect connection. But mostly they were just... passing by. Each performing their own act, never quite managing to hold on."

He broke off a piece of bread and dipped it in his stew. "Denis had his gambling, his secret meetings, his fear of what would happen when his money ran out. And Cadence had her music, her social duties, her desperate attempts to be the perfect wife. They were like those trapeze artists, but without the timing, without the trust. Just two people flying through the air, hoping someone would catch them."

The fire crackled in the range, throwing dancing shadows on the walls. Outside, the wind had picked up again, its moaning around the old house adding a melancholy note to Reed's words.

Israel reached across the table and touched Reed's hand briefly. "And now Cadence fall, but you catch her."

"Yes," Reed said. "Though sometimes I wonder who will catch me." He looked up then, meeting Israel's dark eyes in the lamplight, and something passed between them that needed no words.

"In circus," Israel said carefully, "these flying people, they have net below? To catch them if they fall?"

Reed nodded. "Yes. Though in real life, it's harder to see where the safety nets are. Or who they might be."

They sat in silence then. Each was thinking about safety nets, about trust, about the possibility of two people moving in perfect synchronization through the dangerous air.

Chapter 26
Painted Saints
Israel

Israel followed Reed on the stairs to the first floor, each of them holding a lit candle. Shadows danced on the walls, illuminating those faded places where Denis had sold off the most valuable of the portraits. The house settled around them with odd noises—the wind in the chimneys, the shifting of old timbers, the occasional scurrying of unseen creatures in the walls.

The doors to all the rooms were closed, but firelight leaked out from under one door, and when Reed opened it, the chamber was warm and a fire burned low in the grate, casting dancing shadows on the faded wallpaper. The massive four-poster dominated the room, its heavy curtains drawn back to reveal crisp white sheets. A single candle flickered on the bedside table, its light reflecting in the room's tall windows where darkness pressed against the glass.

As Rebecca said, she'd set a fire in only one bedroom and made the bed up with fresh linens. A pile of sheets and pillowcases rested on a lowboy by the wall, in case they were not to share.

Israel stood in the doorway of the room, feeling shy. He remembered the last time he had been naked in front of someone, the way those two men at the brothel had laughed at him and called him too skinny and too hairy.

"Come in, come in," Reed said. "And close the door behind you. You'll let out all the warm air."

Israel's heart beat faster as Reed closed the door behind them. The room felt like a world apart, separated from London, from their daily lives, from everything except this moment.

"Are you warm enough?" Reed asked softly. He moved to the fire and added another log, stirring the embers until flames licked upward.

"Is warmer than many places I have slept," Israel said. He sat on the edge of the bed, running his hand over the smooth linen. "When I first come to London, I share tiny room with two other students. In winter, we sleep close together for warmth."

Reed sat beside him, close enough that their shoulders touched. "And now? Are you comfortable with Ezra and Silas?"

"They are kind to me. But is their home, their life together. I am guest who stay too long."

"You won't always be a guest," Reed said. He took Israel's hand, his thumb stroking over the knuckles. "You have so many gifts—your mind for numbers, your gentle spirit. You'll make your own way."

Israel turned to look at Reed, studying his face in the flickering light. The fine bones, the intelligent eyes, the soft curve of his mouth. "When I see you that first time, in street, I think you are angel sent by God. So beautiful, so kind to poor man handing out brothel flyers."

Reed's free hand came up to cup Israel's cheek. "And I thought you were a sign that I wasn't alone, that there were others who understood poetry, who saw beauty in words the way I did."

They sat in silence for a moment, the fire crackling softly. The wind had picked up outside, rattling the windows, making their shelter seem even more intimate.

"I am afraid," Israel whispered finally. "Afraid of feeling so much. Last time I touch another man, I lose everything. My studies, my place in community, my future."

Israel breathed in Reed's scent, drawing strength from his warmth. "Torah say man shall not lie with man. When rabbi catch me, he say I betray not just community, but God himself." His voice broke. "All my life, I try to be good Jew. Study hard, follow laws. But this thing inside me..."

"Perhaps God made you exactly as you were meant to be," Reed murmured into Israel's hair.

"I still feel Him here." Israel pressed his hand to his heart. "Still love Him. But maybe... maybe He is bigger than what rabbis say. Maybe His love is bigger too." He looked up at Reed, eyes shining. "When I am with you, I feel close to divine, not far from it. Is that blasphemy?"

"If this is blasphemy," Reed whispered, "then it's the most holy thing I've ever known."

Reed's voice was thick with emotion. "I understand that fear, my dear," Reed said. "When I was discovered, I lost my position, my reputation, very nearly my freedom. But I won't let anyone hurt you that way again."

Israel leaned into Reed's touch, letting himself be held, be comforted. He felt Reed's heart beating against his chest, strong and steady. The candle guttered in a draft, sending shadows dancing across the ceiling.

"Tell me poem," Israel said softly. "Like we talk about that first day."

Reed's voice was gentle in the darkness. "'A thing of beauty is a joy forever: Its loveliness increases; it will never pass into nothingness...' Do you remember?"

"Keats," Israel said, smiling. "I remember everything about that day."

The fire settled with a soft crash of embers, reminding them of where they were—alone in this great empty house, with secrets and dangers swirling around them, but for now safe in this room, in this moment, together.

Reed used his index finger to turn Israel's face toward him. "Is this all right?" he asked as he leaned forward.

"Yes," Israel said, and they kissed. First it was just the feathering of lips against each other, but then the passion overtook them and they crashed their mouths together as if the kiss represented their life's breaths.

The heat in the room, and from Reed's kiss, made Israel warm, and he backed away, pulling off his jumper. Reed did the same with his waistcoat and then, daringly, his shirt. A few blond hairs gathered at his throat, and Israel gasped with pleasure to see them.

He kept his shirt on, though. "My body not like yours," he said. He ran his hand over Reed's upper arm. "So beautiful. Me, I am like bear. Skinny bear. Not handsome."

"I disagree," Reed said. He took Israel's other hand in his and kissed the fingers. "There is soul in your eyes and kindness in the way your lips arch. I want to see all of you, to drink you in like fine wine."

Israel blushed but he did not resist as Reed unbuttoned his shirt. He still wore the tzitzit underneath, but his arms were bare as Reed pulled the shirt from his shoulders. He looked down at the fine brown hairs that coated his arms. Would Reed be repulsed?

"These are the arms of a man," Reed said, running his hands gently down them. "Sometimes I think my body is more like a boy's because I have so little body hair."

"No, you are man," Israel said, his voice hitching.

They leaned together and kissed again, and Israel's cock felt like it had a life of its own, pulsing and pushing forward against his shorts and trousers.

"Enough of this torture," Reed said. He stepped back from Israel. "I need to feel your body against mine." In a quick movement, he pulled his undershirt over his head, and Israel marveled at the planes of his shoulders, the roundness of his upper chest, the flatness of his stomach. A thin trail of blonde hair led down to his waist.

Israel felt he had no choice but to copy Reed. He pulled the fringes out from his belt and took off the tzitzit, exposing his skinny, hairy chest. This was when Reed would pull back, he was sure. But instead Reed leaned forward and grasped Israel's right nipple with his teeth. Israel groaned and his cock pulsed.

Then Reed's hands were all over him, rubbing his chest, squeezing and caressing. Emboldened, Israel undid his flies and let his trousers fall to the floor, then kicked off his shoes and stepped clear.

Reed dropped to his knees on the worn carpet and licked Israel's cock through the fabric of the shorts that Silas had deemed too thin and worn. The pleasure that rose through his body was so strong he could barely stand.

Then Reed stood and shucked the rest of his clothing. In the firelight, he looked to Israel like the embodiment of God, so handsome and loving. Israel leaned down and pulled off his socks, then dropped the thin undershorts to the floor.

They stood like that for a moment in the flickering firelight, each drinking in the other man's body. Unlike when he had bared himself for Louise and her customers, Israel had no fear or shame, only the sense of great good fortune to have this handsome man across from him, regarding him with lust and affection.

Then as one, they moved toward each other, arms reaching out, torsos touching, then their cocks pressed against their bellies. As the fire warmed them, tiny beads of sweat dripped, and the pressure of their rutting increased. Reed pressed against him, and Israel responded with the same force, their bodies slipping and sliding from their sweat and their own lubrication.

The fire's warmth played across their bare skin. Israel breathed in Reed's scent of soap and wool and male musk. Through the window, moonlight silvered Reed's hair and caught the sheen of sweat on his shoulders.

Israel tasted salt on Reed's neck, felt the pulse jumping beneath his tongue. He could not hold out for long as the pressure inside him built. He heard himself make noises he had never made before, deep whimpers of passion that rose from his groin and made their way out his mouth. Then suddenly, Reed spent against his stomach, and that spurred Israel to spend himself.

Reed leaned against Israel's shoulder and nipped at the skin there. "That was amazing," he said.

"Yes, amazing," Israel echoed, leaning his head back to give Reed access to his neck. They were still pressed together, their sticky spend connecting them.

Eventually, though, Reed pulled back. "We need to sleep," he said. He turned and walked toward the ewer on the stand by the door, and Israel was awed at the perfection of his back and arse. In Warsaw once he had entered a Catholic church and been embarrassed at his response to the portrait of naked saints on the walls—their cocks hanging free, their arses round as peaches. Reed could have modeled for any of them.

Reed returned with a wet washcloth and cleaned up the spend on Israel's stomach and groin. He paid particular loving attention to Israel's cock. Then he cleaned himself.

Candle smoke mingled with the cedar scent from the wardrobe. Their skin stuck slightly where they touched, like pages of a damp book. The mattress creaked beneath them, and somewhere in the house a clock chimed midnight.

"And now to bed," Reed said. He walked over to the large four-poster and turned down the covers. Then he slid inside and patted the space next to him.

Israel followed his lead, sliding into the most comfortable wonderful bed he had ever experienced. He turned on his side and Reed pulled him close, spooning against him. Reed was asleep quickly but Israel stayed awake in the moonlight for a while, thinking of all that he had been denied in the past, and all that the future might hold.

Chapter 27
Precise Records
Reed

Reed woke to weak March sunlight filtering through the heavy curtains. His arm was draped across Israel's chest, and for a moment he allowed himself to savor the warmth and closeness. But the fire had died down during the night, and the room was cold. And there was work to be done.

They used the water from the ewer and basin once again to hurriedly clean themselves. Then they dressed and went down for breakfast. Reed lit a fire in the kitchen and made tea for them, and they were sitting at the kitchen table drinking when Mrs. Thompson arrived with bread and cheese and her homemade jam for their breakfast.

"Himself will be in the estate office when you're ready," she said. "The small cottage down by the river."

They thanked her, ate quickly, and walked through the dew-laden field to the cottage. The morning sun took some of the chill out of the air.

The office was a small room warmed by a pot-bellied stove. Maps lined the walls, showing the boundaries of Drayton House's lands, and a large ledger lay open on a sturdy oak table. The morning light filtered through windows clouded with years of agricultural dust.

Reed sat between Israel and Thompson, breathing in the mingled scents of coal smoke and leather bindings. He looked at Israel, whose fingers seemed to itch to touch the ledger's pages, to immerse himself in the columns of figures that would tell the estate's story.

"I keep precise records," Thompson said, opening the most recent volume. "Though his lordship rarely looked at them this past year."

Israel leaned forward, his eyes moving rapidly over the entries. "You separate income by source," he said. "Is very good method, what my uncle use."

Thompson looked surprised at Israel's interest. "Yes, exactly. Here's the dairy income—we produce mainly cheese. Then the tenant farmers' rents, the orchard proceeds, the wool profits..."

"May I?" Israel asked, pulling the ledger closer. He began to add figures in his head, his lips moving slightly as he calculated. Reed watched him with amusement as the familiar dance of numbers calmed him, helping him forget whatever nervousness he had about being in a grand house.

"Israel has quite a gift for mathematics," he explained to Thompson.

"I see pattern here," Israel said suddenly. "Each month, income drop little bit. Is steady decline." He pointed to the figures. "In March last year, total income was three hundred forty-two pounds, four shillings. By December, only two hundred ninety-one pounds, eighteen shillings."

Thompson nodded grimly. "That would be the land sales. His lordship sold off three farms and a portion of the woodland."

"But remaining lands still produce good income," Israel said. He turned back several pages, comparing figures. "Even with repairs needed, house can support itself. If..." he hesitated, glancing at Reed.

"Go on," Reed encouraged.

"If gambling stops. If no more sales." Israel ran his finger down a column. "Cheese production alone brings twenty-eight pounds each month. Tenant rents another hundred fifty. Wool and timber rights add more."

The Lord's Gambit

Thompson pulled out a stack of papers. "These are the repair estimates I've gathered. The roof, the water damage, the north wing..."

Israel took them, his quick mind already calculating. "Yes, is expensive. But can be done over time, if prioritize worst problems first." He looked up at Thompson. "You have schedule of most urgent repairs?"

The estate manager's initial wariness seemed to fade as he recognized Israel's expertise. "Here," he said, pulling out another sheet. "The water damage in the east corridor needs immediate attention. Then the north wing roof before next winter."

Reed watched as Israel began writing figures on a clean sheet of paper, creating a timeline of necessary repairs matched against projected income. His hand moved swiftly, setting up columns and rows with practiced ease. "If house keep current income, and no more debts added, repairs can be completed in eighteen months."

For the first time in a long time, Reed felt his nervousness ease. It had been the right move to bring Israel along, and now they could see light at the end of the tunnel.

Reed leaned closer to examine Israel's calculations. "Are you certain?"

"I am certain of math," Israel said. "But not certain of people. Cannot predict if more bills will come, or if more land will be sold."

He turned back to the ledger. "The estate has good bones. Is like man who is sick but not dying. Need proper care, good food, time to heal."

"And no more bleeding," Reed added quietly, his meaning clear to Israel if not to Thompson.

They spent the rest of the morning going through the accounts in detail. Reed and Israel created a complete financial picture, noting every source of income and every regular expense. Their concentration was total; they barely noticed when Rebecca brought them tea and thick slices of seed cake.

By the time darkness began to fall, Israel had filled several pages with neat columns of figures, each telling part of the estate's story.

"You do fine job here," he told Thompson as they prepared to leave. "Books are clear, honest. Easy to see where money come from, where it go."

The estate manager seemed pleased by the praise. "Thank you, Mr. Kupersmit. I must say, you've helped me understand our position much better. Sometimes looking at the same figures day after day, one misses the larger pattern."

As they walked back to the house for dinner, Reed touched Israel's arm lightly. "You were brilliant in there," he said softly. "I think you've given us all hope that the estate can be saved."

"Numbers give me solid ground under feet," he said.

"And I hope I have given you something solid as well," Reed said, knocking his hip against Israel's.

They settled in the kitchen when Rebecca arrived with dinner. After she left, Reed looked through the cabinets. "What you look for?"

"Just curious to see what's here," Reed said. Then he spotted what he wanted—a small jar of kitchen grease. He turned his back to Israel and slid it into his pocket.

In the flickering firelight, Reed watched Israel eat, marveling at how he had grown and changed since their first meeting. Even after their intimacy the night before, these quiet moments stirred something deeper in him—a longing not just for Israel's body, but for his gentle spirit.

"What cause that smile?" Israel asked, catching Reed's gaze.

"I was thinking how remarkable you are," Reed said softly. "Most men see only figures on a page. You see stories, patterns, the pulse of life beneath the numbers."

Israel ducked his head, a blush creeping up his neck. "Is nothing special. Just way my mind works."

"Everything about you is special." Reed moved closer, drawn by the warmth in Israel's dark eyes. "Do you know, when we first met, I

The Lord's Gambit

thought Providence had sent you to me? There I was, feeling utterly alone in London, and suddenly there was this beautiful man who could quote Keats and understand poetry's power to transform the soul."

"You saw me when I was lowest," Israel whispered. "Dirty, hungry, ashamed. Yet you treated me like gentleman."

"You were always a gentleman. The circumstances couldn't hide your true nature." Reed reached out to touch Israel's cheek, his thumb brushing over the spot where the payess had once curled. "Just as they couldn't hide your grace, your kindness, the light in your eyes when you speak of things that move you."

Israel leaned into the touch. "With you, I feel... how to say? Like puzzle piece that finally finds right place. All corners match perfect."

Reed felt his heart swell at the simple poetry of those words. "Yes," he breathed. "Exactly that." He leaned forward until their foreheads touched, breathing in the subtle spice of Israel's soap, the warmth of his skin. "I never thought I would find someone who fits so perfectly."

The fire crackled behind them, casting dancing shadows on the walls. In that moment, the grand house with all its troubles seemed to fade away, leaving only this—two souls finding harbor in each other after long journeys through storm-tossed seas.

They climbed the stairs together, holding hands, and this time both of them knew what was coming. They stripped their clothes quickly, and stood facing each other in the moonlight.

"I see what you take from kitchen," Israel said with a smile. "It is for bedroom, yes?"

"Yes, but only if you wish," Reed said. He pulled Israel close and they kissed, their lips so close together they were sharing breath. Reed's cock was stiff and so was Israel's, and the reached down to Israel's buttocks and pulled him close.

"You still need some meat back there," he said.

Israel's eyes glinted with humor. "You mean meat like sausage?" He reached down and gripped Reed's cock.

Reed laughed, even as desire rushed through his body. "That wasn't what I meant, but we can do that if you like."

"I have never," Israel said. "But I have heard men do that. You have?"

"Once or twice, at school," Reed said. "Mostly older, bigger boys used me that way. But I liked it, and I think you might."

"I trust you," Israel said, and those words were like a spear to Reed's heart. This man, who had been so ill-used in the past, trusted him with intimacy.

"It's easier if we lie down together," Reed said. He directed Israel onto the bed, on his side. He retrieved the pot of grease from his trouser pocket and applied some to his index finger. "Tell me if this hurts."

He lay down beside Israel, his front to Israel's back, and caressed the fine hairs that surrounded Israel's hole. Israel giggled. Then Reed touched the rosebud that lay beneath the hair with the tip of his finger, and Israel's body tensed.

"Is that all right?" Reed whispered.

"Is good," Israel said. "More, please."

"Yes, sir," Reed said, and those words reminded him of an encounter he'd had with a captain in the Navy, when he'd said those same words. How gentle the captain had been with him, how much pleasure the older man had brought him. He was determined to do the same for Israel.

Cautiously he moved his finger forward, and it was like Israel's body welcomed him, pulling him forward. "Is nice," Israel said.

Reed pried Israel's cheeks open and added a second finger, and then a third. Israel rocked and whimpered beneath him, and Reed pulled his fingers back.

"Why you stop?" Israel asked, his voice partly muffled by his face against the pillow.

"Because there is something better to come," Reed said. He took more grease from the pot and rubbed it down his cock, then once again pried Israel's cheeks apart. A tiny bit of grease dripped from Israel's hole, which was open and welcoming.

Reed positioned himself on the bed so he could have easiest access, and slipped his cock up to Israel's hole, then pushed the tip inside. "Oh," Israel moaned.

Gradually, Reed inched forward. "If it hurts, tell me," he said.

"Hurts but good," Israel said. "I want it."

With a final push, Reed was inside, the head of his cock up against what he thought was Israel's prostate. "Is this all right, my love?" Reed asked.

"More than all right," Israel said. He clenched the muscles of his buttocks around Reed's cock, and Reed gasped. They began a rhythm of in and out, clench and unclench, until Reed thought he would pass out from the ecstasy.

Israel seemed to be enjoying himself as well. He reached down and grasped his cock and stroked it with the rhythm of Reed's insertion, and he spent against the sheets a moment before Reed could no longer hold back, and let himself go.

It was a moment of the most exquisite communion. Reed had enjoyed sex before but he had never felt such a connection to another man. This, this, was what he was destined for. This link to Israel. In a revelation, he knew he would do whatever he could to retain it.

Chapter 28
Urgent Summons
Israel

The next morning, it was Thompson who delivered their breakfast. After he'd laid out the food on the table, he said, "There's something else about his lordship's visitors." He motioned to a chair. "If I may join you?"

"Certainly," Reed said. "This porridge can wait."

"Wasn't sure whether to mention it, but seeing as you're investigating..." Israel watched as the estate manager pulled a small notebook from his pocket, the kind used for recording crop yields and rainfall. "I kept track of them," Thompson said. "Dates, times. Seemed prudent, though his lordship never knew."

Thompson spread the notebook on the desk. Israel noticed his hands were trembling slightly.

"First time was last summer. Three men came late at night—Lord Ashworth, who I recognized from the House of Lords, a man I heard called Commodore Aiken, and a foreign gentleman, Hungarian I think, named Professor Varga."

"I know of Commodore Aiken," Reed said. "When I was in the Navy, I served on a ship under his command."

Israel leaned forward to look at Thompson's careful notations.

The dates aligned perfectly with some of the payments he'd found in Denis's ledgers.

"They'd meet in the library," Thompson continued. "Sometimes until dawn. His lordship would have me bring them coffee and brandy, then wait up to make sure no one approached the house."

"What did they discuss?" Reed asked quietly.

"Couldn't hear much. But once, when I was bringing more coffee, I heard them talking about Russian expansion in Central Asia. Professor Varga was saying something about intelligence from Budapest about railway lines being built toward India."

Israel saw Reed's body stiffen slightly at this information.

"The strange thing was," Thompson said, "after these meetings, his lordship would go to London and lose heavily at cards. Deliberately, mind you. I once heard him tell Lord Ashworth, 'Another ten thousand ought to do it. Litvinov's getting eager.'"

"You think he lose on purpose?" Israel asked.

Thompson nodded. "And more than that. Two weeks before he died, I heard him tell Commodore Aiken, 'The fish is nearly hooked. We'll have proof of everything soon.'" Thompson's voice dropped. "Next day, Professor Varga arrived alone. They argued in the library. I heard the professor say something about their position being compromised, that someone had talked."

"When was the last meeting?" Reed asked.

"Three days before his lordship died. All of them came—Ashworth, Aiken, Varga. They burned papers in the library fireplace. His lordship seemed frightened. Not his usual self at all." Thompson swallowed hard. "Next morning, he asked me to look after her ladyship if anything happened to him. I thought he was just in one of his dark moods."

Thompson stood, pulling something from his boot. "Found this under the library floorboards yesterday, when I was checking for rot." He handed Reed a small key. "I believe that it matches a strongbox in his lordship's London house. Didn't seem right to mention it until I was sure you were... well, on the right side of things."

The Lord's Gambit

Israel watched as Reed processed this information, seeing the subtle changes in his expression. He was distracted by the way Reed's fingers handled the delicate china teacup, imagining those elegant hands cupped around his face. The morning light caught the gold in Reed's hair, and Israel noticed how his collar had loosened slightly, revealing the pale hollow of his throat. When Reed reached across the desk for more papers, the fabric of his shirt pulled taut across his shoulders, and Israel had to look away, his breath catching.

Reed seemed similarly affected. His eyes lingered on Israel's hands as they sorted through documents, on the way Israel's dark curls fell across his forehead when he bent to examine figures.

Thompson pushed his chair back and stood. "I'll let you get to your breakfast, then." He walked out, and Reed and Israel hurried through their porridge and took the key and the notebook to Denis's office.

Israel sat at the desk, surrounded by ledgers and correspondence, and settled into the methodical work that he loved. Reed sat nearby, sorting through a pile of papers they had found in Denis's safe. The fire crackled in the grate, barely keeping the morning chill at bay.

Every time Reed leaned over to examine a document Israel was holding, his breath warmed Israel's neck. The scent of his cologne, sandalwood and citrus, made it difficult for Israel to focus on the numbers before him. Their fingers brushed as they passed papers back and forth, each touch sending sparks through Israel's body.

He caught Reed watching him, admiring the way he rapidly calculated figures in his head. The pride in Reed's eyes made Israel's cheeks warm. When Reed's hand rested on the back of his chair, fingers just barely touching Israel's shoulder, Israel had to suppress a shiver of pleasure at the casual intimacy.

They maintained perfect propriety, speaking only of accounts and evidence. But their eyes met often across the desk, carrying messages of desire and affection that needed no words.

"Look at this," Israel said suddenly. "Is strange." He pulled several documents from different piles and laid them side by side.

"Here, Litvinov lend Denis two thousand pounds. Same day, Denis pay same amount to Colin Sinclair."

Reed leaned over to look. "That's not unusual. Denis probably borrowed from Litvinov to pay another debt."

"No, is more." Israel's fingers traced down columns of figures. "Happen again next month. Three thousand from Litvinov, three thousand to Sinclair. But look at these." He pulled out the IOUs they had found the day before. "Numbers match exactly, every time. Same day, same amount."

"Perhaps Sinclair was the gambler Denis owed?"

Israel shook his head. "No, man at gambling hall tell you Denis pay debts there. In ledger, Sinclair payments listed under 'consulting fees.'"

"What do you make of that?"

"Not sure yet." Israel spread more papers across the desk. "But pattern continue. Every payment from Litvinov match exactly with payment to Sinclair. Is too perfect to be accident."

When their fingers brushed over a ledger, Reed's breath hitched audibly. The air between them grew thick with unspoken desire.

"These numbers," Israel said, his voice husky. "They swim before my eyes."

"Perhaps we need a break," Reed suggested, his own voice unsteady. But neither moved, caught in the magnetic pull between them.

There was a knock on the door, and Reed answered. "I thought you gentlemen might need refreshment," Mrs. Thompson said.

After she left, Reed spread a thick layer of cream on a scone and held it to Israel's lips. "You're too thin," he said softly. "Let me feed you."

Israel's mouth opened, accepting both the sweet offering and the intimacy of being cared for. The cream melted on his tongue as Reed's fingers brushed his lips.

By the time they finished, they were sated. But before they could go back to work, they heard the sound of hooves in the drive. A few

The Lord's Gambit

moments later, Thompson knocked on the office door, slightly out of breath.

"Telegram from London, sir," he said, handing Reed a yellow envelope. "Special messenger just rode out from Gloucester. Said he was instructed to wait for a reply."

Reed tore open the envelope, his face growing grave as he read. "It's from Wigton," he said. "There's been some kind of trouble. He needs us back in London immediately." He looked up at Thompson. "Could you arrange a carriage to take us to the station? We'll need to catch the next train."

"There's one at two o'clock," Thompson said. "I'll send word to Harry Willcox. His horses are fastest."

"And tell the messenger to reply, "ARRIVING SOONEST STOP LYDNEY."

After Thompson left, Reed handed the telegram to Israel. The message was brief: "RETURN URGENT STOP LITVINOV MAKING DEMANDS STOP CADENCE DISTRAUGHT STOP WIGTON."

"We must take these papers," Israel said, gathering up the documents showing the pattern he'd discovered. "Maybe important."

"Yes," Reed agreed. "Though I don't understand how yet." He began helping Israel sort through the papers, their hands occasionally brushing. Despite the urgency of the moment, Israel felt a thrill at each touch, remembering the night before.

They worked quickly to pack what they needed, while Rebecca prepared some food for their journey. Israel gathered up their papers while Reed questioned Thompson about where exactly in the London house they might find this strongbox.

As they hurried out to the waiting carriage, Israel's mind was racing. The columns of numbers in Denis's ledger weren't just records of gambling debts—they were coding something else entirely. Something that had gotten Denis killed.

"You think Denis work for Foreign Office?" he asked Reed quietly as they settled into the carriage.

"Or a private group trying to counter Russian influence," Reed replied. "Either way, it seems my brother-in-law was playing a very dangerous game."

Israel clutched his satchel of documents closer. Hidden in these innocent-looking columns of figures might be the key to understanding not just Denis's death, but something much larger. Something worth killing for.

Reed noticed Israel shivering slightly in the chill air. Without comment, he removed his own wool scarf and gently wrapped it around Israel's neck. His fingers lingered for a moment against Israel's throat, adjusting the soft fabric.

"But you will be cold," Israel protested softly.

"I'm quite warm enough," Reed said. He hesitated, then added quietly, "My mother knitted this scarf for me, the winter before she died. Sometimes wearing it feels like still having her love wrapped around me." He smiled. "Now it can keep you warm as well."

Israel touched the scarf reverently. "To share something so precious..."

"You are precious to me," Reed whispered, so softly it was almost lost in the rattle of the sound of the carriage wheels on the gravel outside. Their eyes met in the dim light, and for a moment all the intrigue and danger fell away, leaving only this, two souls finding harbor in each other.

Harry Willcox's fast pair would get them to Gloucester in plenty of time for the two o'clock train. As they rode, something about those matching payments nagged at Israel. He had a feeling the answer was right in front of them, if only they could see it.

The carriage set off at a brisk pace, the wheels clattering on the drive. Israel glanced back at Drayton House, its honey-colored stone glowing in the midday sun. So many secrets in those walls, he thought. But perhaps the most important ones were here in his lap, hidden in columns of numbers that told a story he was only beginning to understand.

"What you think Litvinov want?" he asked Reed quietly.

The Lord's Gambit

"I don't know," Reed replied. "But whatever it is, we have to protect Cadence." His hand found Israel's, hidden by the carriage blanket. "And each other."

Israel squeezed Reed's hand, drawing strength from the connection. Whatever awaited them in London, they would face it together.

Chapter 29
Vital Documents
Reed

When they arrived at Bloomsbury Square, they found Wigton pacing the salon while Cadence sat rigid in a chair, her face pale. She held a letter in trembling hands.

"Thank God you're back," Wigton said. "It arrived this morning by special messenger."

Reed took the letter from Cadence. The paper was heavy, expensive, with a watermark he recognized from the IOUs they'd found at Drayton House. Litvinov's elegant script was precise and threatening:

"My dear Lady Harlow,

Your late husband removed certain documents from my possession, using them to guarantee his considerable debts to me. These must be returned within three days, or I shall be forced to reveal to London society that the Countess of Harlow's finances are in such disarray that she has been entertaining gentleman callers during her period of mourning to raise funds. I have witnesses who will attest to seeing Mr. Wigton emerge from your bedroom.

The scandal would, of course, destroy any chance of you maintaining your position in society. I would hate to see such a lovely young woman cast out, forced to rely on the charity of others.

Perhaps even forced into the kind of establishment your brother is known to frequent.

Return what is mine, and all will be forgotten.

Yours most sincerely,

S. Litvinov"

Reed's hands shook with rage as he turned to Wigton. "Tell me he's lying."

"Of course he is," Wigton said. "I've never been anywhere near her ladyship's bedroom. But in the current climate, with Lord Harlow's suicide so fresh in everyone's minds…"

"The scandal would ruin her," Reed finished. He turned to Israel. "The key Thompson gave us. Could Denis have hidden whatever Litvinov wants in that strongbox?"

They left Cadence in the salon, with Mrs. Clarkson to comfort her. They hurried to Denis's office, where Reed began feeling along the wainscoting as Thompson had described. Behind a loose panel, he found a small iron strongbox.

Reed's hands shook as he inserted the key. The lock turned with difficulty, as if it hadn't been opened in some time. Inside, they found a stack of documents and a small leather notebook.

The documents were in the Cyrillic alphabet. "Can you read these?" he asked Israel. "Is it like Polish?"

Israel shook his head. "No, alphabets are different. Polish use same alphabet as English. But back home, many documents come from Russia, so I learn."

He examined the first paper. "Official letterhead, from Russian Railway Ministry. I don't know all words, but see this letter P, with two lines at bottom? Is for rubles." He flipped to the next pages. "And look—maps of Central Asia with routes marked in red ink."

Reed picked up the notebook. Denis's familiar scrawl filled the pages, but it wasn't in English. "Some kind of code," he said. "No,

The Lord's Gambit

wait." He looked closer. "It's a mix of languages. French, German... something else."

Wigton looked over his shoulder. "That's Hungarian," he said. "We had a nanny when I was a boy who was from Budapest. I learned some of the language from her. These are details about railway construction, troop movements, and arms shipments."

"Denis was spy?" Israel asked softly.

"Not exactly," Reed said, continuing to read. "He was part of a group monitoring Russian expansion toward India. These railway documents... they prove that Russia is preparing military infrastructure, disguised as commercial development." He turned more pages. "And Litvinov... good God."

"What is it?"

"Litvinov wasn't just a moneylender. He was using gambling debts to control votes in Parliament, just as Gervase Quinn feared."

Wigton followed his finger down the list. "Every lord he brought under his influence would have a vote against any measure to check Russian expansion."

"Denis and his friends must have been gathering evidence against him," Reed said. "Notice whose name is not on the list? Lord Ashton, who Thompson at Drayton House said was one of three men who visited Denis there."

He looked up at them. "He told us that the last time a Professor Varga visited, three days before Denis's suicide, warned that their network had been compromised."

"That why Denis kill himself?" Israel asked. "Because Litvinov discover what he do?"

Reed shook his head. "I don't think Denis killed himself at all. Look at this last entry, dated the day he died: 'L suspects. Must get evidence to A. If anything happens to me, Thompson has key.'"

"A must be Lord Ashworth," Israel said. "Thompson say he was leader."

"Or Commodore Aiken," Reed said. "Both of them could be A."

"And now Litvinov thinks we have this evidence, which we do," Wigton said. "But what do we do with it?"

Reed gathered the documents quickly. "We need to get these to the Foreign Office immediately. Gervase Quinn will know what to do."

"But Litvinov's threat—"

"Will be meaningless once he's arrested as a foreign agent. Even the suggestion that he attempted to blackmail a peer's widow would destroy him in London society." Reed touched Israel's arm. "You found the pattern in his payments that helped us understand all this. Denis's mathematical code in his ledgers."

"We save Cadence together," Israel said simply.

Reed wanted nothing more than to take Israel in his arms, but Wigton was there, and there would be time for that later. Right now, they had to get these documents to safety. He gathered everything into his briefcase, then stood. "Come. Let's go tell my sister that her husband wasn't just a dissolute gambler after all. And then we'll finish what he started."

As they walked back to the salon, Reed felt the weight of the documents in his briefcase. Denis had died trying to protect Britain's interests. The least they could do was ensure his death wasn't in vain.

Chapter 30
Rush to Judgment
Israel

They decided that Antony Wigton would remain with Cadence while Reed and Israel went to the Foreign Office.

Israel struggled to keep up with Reed as they hurried through the late afternoon streets toward Whitehall. The briefcase that held Denis's documents bumped against Reed's leg as he strode forward with purpose, while Israel felt like a shadow, trying to stay close.

The Foreign Office loomed ahead, its white stone facade darkened by London smoke. A posse of well-dressed men descended the steps, their top hats gleaming in the weak sunlight, and Israel's heart began to race. Every bobby they passed made him want to turn and run. He had spent so long avoiding official notice, and now he was walking directly into the belly of the beast.

Reed must have sensed his hesitation, because he dropped back and squeezed Israel's arm. "It will be fine," he said. "Quinn is a reasonable man."

But would he be reasonable to a Polish Jew whose English was barely passable? Israel's stomach churned as they climbed the steps. Inside, the floor was inlaid with an intricate pattern of blue and cream tiles, and the ceiling soared above them. Their footsteps echoed as a uniformed porter directed them to Quinn's office.

Israel had never seen such grandeur as the carved wooden banisters on the stairs, the brass gas fixtures, the numbered doors with frosted glass panels. Men hurried past them carrying leather portfolios and dispatch cases, speaking in cultured accents that Israel could barely understand.

Quinn's office was at the top of the building. The window behind his desk looked out over the street, and Israel saw the towers of Westminster Abbey in the distance. Quinn himself was exactly as Reed had described him, tall and lean, with an air of quiet authority.

He looked up as they entered, his eyes flickering over Israel before settling on Reed. "Lydney. What brings you here at this hour?"

"We've found something." Reed placed the briefcase on Quinn's desk. "The evidence you wanted that Sergei Litvinov is working to influence votes in Parliament on behalf of Russian interests."

Quinn's eyebrows rose as Reed explained about Denis's role in gathering intelligence, and the documents they had discovered. Israel watched as the Quinn examined the papers, his expression growing more grave with each page he turned.

"This is exactly what we needed," Quinn said finally. "But we must move carefully. Litvinov has many friends in high places."

"He's threatening my sister," Reed said. "Trying to blackmail her into returning these documents."

Quinn nodded slowly. "Then we use that. Set up a meeting. Tell him you've found what he wants and will exchange it for leaving your sister alone. We'll have men in place to arrest him when he arrives."

"Where should this meeting take place?" Reed asked.

"Somewhere public enough that he'll feel safe coming alone, but private enough for our purposes." Quinn thought for a moment. "The Palm Court at the Langham Hotel. Tomorrow evening at eight. We'll have men positioned in the lobby and the restaurant."

As the two men worked out the details, Israel felt increasingly invisible. What was his role in all this? He had spent enough time in London to know that Jews, especially foreign-born ones like himself, were often convenient scapegoats when the authorities needed someone to blame.

Even with his newly trimmed appearance and proper English clothes, his accent and background marked him as an outsider. The Foreign Office might find it simpler to pin some minor part of the conspiracy on him rather than face uncomfortable questions about English lords working as spies.

Reed must have sensed his discomfort. "Mr. Kupersmit was instrumental in uncovering the pattern in Lord Harlow's accounts," he said to Quinn. "Without his mathematical skills, we might never have understood what we were seeing."

Quinn's sharp eyes assessed Israel once more. "Indeed? Perhaps we could make use of such skills in the future."

Israel's heart leaped. Was that an offer of employment? But no, surely not. He was just a poor immigrant, barely able to speak proper English.

"For now," Quinn continued, "I suggest you both go home and get some rest. Tomorrow will be a challenging day." He began writing in a small notebook. "I'll have a message sent round in the morning with the final details."

As they walked back down the grand staircase, Israel felt Reed's hand brush against his. "You were very brave," Reed murmured. "I know how difficult that must have been for you."

Israel managed a small smile. "Is like going into lion's den. But Daniel survive that, yes? Perhaps I survive this too."

Reed's answering smile warmed him. "More than survive, I hope. Quinn was impressed by you, though he's too proper to show it directly."

Outside, the gas lamps were being lit along Whitehall, and a thin fog was rolling in from the river. Israel took a deep breath of the damp air, grateful to be out of that imposing building.

"Come," Reed said. "We should tell Cadence what's happening. Then perhaps..." He hesitated. "Perhaps you could stay with us tonight? It might be safer than returning to Hackney."

Israel nodded, his heart lifting despite his lingering fears. Whatever tomorrow might bring, at least he would face it with Reed beside him.

They hurried back to Bloomsbury Square, where they found Cadence and Wigton waiting anxiously in the salon.

Chapter 31
Precious Friendship
Reed

Reed watched his sister's face as he explained what would happen the next evening at the Langham. She was pale but composed, finally understanding that her late husband had been more than the dissolute gambler she had imagined. Wigton sat beside her – that afternoon they had been properly chaperoned by Mrs. Clarkson's presence in the adjoining room - and Reed noticed how he leaned toward Cadence when she spoke, as if drawn by an invisible thread.

"It seems too simple," Cadence said, twisting her handkerchief. "Surely Litvinov will suspect a trap?"

"I believe that's what Quinn is counting on," Wigton said. "That Litvinov's arrogance will lead him to believe he can outsmart whatever trap that has been set."

Mrs. Clarkson had outdone herself with dinner that evening, perhaps sensing that something momentous had occurred. The dining room glowed with candlelight, and she had set out the best Spode china with its blue Italian pattern.

The four of them sat to dinner together. "I still don't understand how you discovered the pattern in Lord Harlow's accounts," Wigton said, reaching for the claret. "That seems to have been the key to everything."

"That was Israel's discovery," Reed said. He felt a warmth spread through him at just speaking the name. "His gift for mathematics revealed what we all missed - the careful coding of payments that pointed to Denis's true activities."

Over bread pudding, Israel watched Reed's hands - so elegant with the silver spoon, yet he had seen them shake with fear at the Foreign Office. Those same hands had touched him with such tenderness.

"You are quite remarkable," Cadence said, turning to Israel. "When Reed first brought you here I thought you very foreign, very timid. But there's a quiet strength to you."

Israel blushed and lowered his head.

"Yes." Reed took a sip of wine to steady himself. "In fact, I believe my first meeting with Israel was ordained by Providence."

"The day you bought him tea?" Cadence asked. "You never did tell us the whole story."

Reed smiled, and under the table he took Israel's hand. "I found him on the street that bitter January day. We discovered a mutual love of poetry, Keats in particular. He had learned English partially by reading *Endymion*." He looked at Israel. "I never expected to find someone who understood both the beauty of words and the stories numbers can tell."

When he looked back at his sister and his friend, he saw understanding in both their faces. Wigton's expression was particularly knowing. After all, they had been at school together, and had shared confidences in the past.

"A friend like that is precious indeed," Wigton said carefully. "One might even say... special."

"Very special," Reed agreed, meeting his old friend's eyes. He squeezed Israel's hand under the table, then released it.

Cadence smiled across the table. "I'm so glad you've found

someone who appreciates your fine qualities, dear brother. Someone who sees you as clearly as you see him."

The acceptance in her voice made Reed's throat tight. "As clearly as Wigton sees you, perhaps?"

A blush rose in Cadence's cheeks, but she didn't pull her hand away. "Perhaps," she said softly. "Though of course nothing can come of that until my period of mourning is complete."

"Of course not," Wigton said. But his eyes never left her face.

They finished their dinner in companionable silence, each lost in thoughts of connections found and futures glimpsed. Reed raised his glass.

"To special friendships," he said, and Israel echoed him.

"To understanding hearts," Cadence added.

"To patience," Wigton said, with a gentle smile at Cadence.

Reed sat back, warmed by more than wine. Tomorrow would bring danger and confrontation, but tonight was for appreciation of these subtle bonds of love and acceptance, wrapped in the careful language of their time but no less real for that.

They talked until the lamps burned low and Mrs. Clarkson had long since retired. Finally, Wigton took his leave, pressing Cadence's hand as he said goodnight. Reed told Cadence of his suggestion that Israel stay at the house, given the late hour and what lay ahead tomorrow. "And your hosts will assume you are still in the country," he added to Israel.

"I think I shall go upstairs, and leave you two time alone," Cadence said, as she rose. "Reed, you will see that Israel has all he needs to spend the night with us?"

Reed nodded. "Good night, sister."

"Good night, brother." She smiled and looked at Israel. "Thank you for everything. I look forward to calling you a dear friend."

"I do also, my lady."

"Please, you must call me Cadence, if we are to be part of the same family someday."

"Cadence, then," Israel said, and Reed liked the way his sister's name sounded in Israel's voice.

She left, and Israel turned to Reed. "I not need much."

"We have a guest room on the third floor," Reed said. "It's not much, but I think it would be better if you stayed up there, rather than in my room."

The house creaked around them as they climbed the stairs, their candles casting dancing shadows. In a patch of moonlight filtering through a window, Reed paused and turned to Israel.

"Your tzitzit," Reed said softly. "I've noticed you still wear it, even after..." He gestured to Israel's clean-shaven face.

Israel's free hand went to his chest, where the garment lay hidden beneath his shirt. "Is reminder," he said. "That some things change, but core remains. Like tree in winter. Leaves fall, but roots stay strong."

Reed set his candle on a windowsill and gently placed his palm over Israel's heart, feeling the fabric beneath. "Your faith is part of who you are. I would never ask you to change that."

"Many things I question now," Israel whispered. "But not this, having someone who sees all parts of me, accepts all parts."

Reed's eyes shone in the candlelight. "As you accept all parts of me."

Mrs. Clarkson had kept the room made up for some time, even though there had been no guests. "I'll light the fire for you, shall I?" Reed asked.

He knelt at the hearth, aware of Israel standing behind him. The kindling caught quickly, and soon flames danced across the coal. Reed remained crouched there a moment longer than necessary, steadying himself before he turned.

Israel stood in the center of the room, looking uncertain yet somehow right - as if he belonged here in this house, in Reed's life. The firelight caught the planes of his face, softening them, and Reed was struck again by how beautiful he was, despite his own doubts about his appearance.

The Lord's Gambit

"Strange to be guest in grand house," Israel said softly. "Never think this happen to me."

Reed crossed to him, taking both his hands. "You're not a guest," he said. "You're..." He paused, searching for the right words. "You're essential. To this case, yes, but more than that. To me."

Israel's dark eyes seemed to glow in the firelight. "I feel same," he whispered. "Like missing piece of self, found at last."

Reed reached up to touch Israel's face, tracing the line of his jaw where the beard had been. "When I first saw you on that street, something in me recognized you. As if my soul knew yours, even then."

"Poetry man," Israel said with a soft smile. "Always such beautiful words."

"Only because you inspire them." Reed leaned forward until their foreheads touched. They stood like that for a long moment, breathing together, while the fire crackled and London's sounds drifted up from the street below.

Tomorrow would bring danger, but tonight they had this - this quiet moment of connection, this sense of having found harbor after a long storm. Reed knew they would have to be careful, maintain proper appearances, but here in this firelit room, they could simply be themselves, two hearts beating in perfect synchronization.

"Tell me," Israel said softly, "what frighten you most about tomorrow?"

Reed considered. "Not Litvinov himself. But that I might fail to protect those I..." He glanced at Israel, then away. "Those I care for."

"Like Cadence."

"Like you." Reed's voice was barely a whisper. "I keep thinking of that day I found you on the street. How close I came to walking past, to missing this chance at..." He gestured between them. "At whatever this precious thing is we've found."

Israel reached across, letting his fingers brush Reed's. "In Hebrew, we say 'bashert,' meant to be. Like when string of fate ties two souls together."

Reed's eyes glistened in the candlelight. "Yes. Exactly that."

Chapter 32
Secrets and Lies
Israel

Israel walked to Pemberton's office at Gray's Inn early Friday morning, still warm from the memories of his night at Bloomsbury Square. Though propriety had required him to sleep in a separate room, just knowing that Reed was under the same roof had filled him with a profound sense of rightness.

Silas was already at his desk, arranging a small vase of hothouse violets. He adjusted each bloom with delicate precision, then turned his attention to aligning his crystal inkwell perfectly parallel to his pen rest. His mauve waistcoat was embroidered with tiny silver threads that caught the morning light.

The office smelled of coal smoke and leather bindings, and Luke sorted through files nearby. When Israel appeared, Silas gestured him to sit. "You look different," Silas said. "Something has changed."

"Many things change," Israel said. "Lord Harlow was good man, not wastrel. He spy on Russians, and tonight we help catch Litvinov."

That got both clerks' attention. Luke abandoned his sorting and drew closer as Israel explained what they had discovered at Drayton House, and about the strongbox.

"Well," Silas said when Israel finished, "that explains what we found about the house on Binney Street." He pulled out a document.

"The property was purchased through a series of companies, each more hidden than last. But final owner is a company called Anglo-Hungarian Trading Limited."

"Hungarian professor!" Israel exclaimed. "Varga, he meet with Lord Harlow at Drayton House."

"Exactly. And there's more." Silas lowered his voice, though Luke had returned to his files. "We found documents showing the owner of the gaming hell, Jasper Fitch, was in on it as well. His sister is married to Professor Varga. When Lord Harlow lost money at certain tables, the money went from Fitch's account to the account of Anglo-Hungarian Trading."

Israel nodded slowly, remembering the peculiar layout of the house on Binney Street. Then he blushed, recalling what he and Reed had done on that very table.

"Listen to this," Silas continued, thankfully missing Israel's discomfort. "The house on Binney Street connects through its cellar to old wine vaults. They run under several buildings in Mayfair, including the Russian Embassy."

Israel's eyes widened. "So Russians hear what happening above?"

Silas shook his head. "No, the other way around. There's a ventilation shaft that goes up through the walls. It is placed perfectly to catch conversations in the Russian Ambassador's private office." Silas pulled out a carefully drawn diagram.

"Do the Russians know this?"

"Not as far as Lord Harlow and his conspirators knew," Silas said. "In the files you left behind, we found a series of plans provided by Commodore Aiken through his contacts in military intelligence. He told his lordship about the way that speaking tubes are used in naval vessels. Plans were drawn up for a network of brass tubes, disguised as ventilation pipes, which ran up through the walls of the Embassy."

Silas pulled out a carefully drawn diagram. "See these marks? They show where the tubes end. One comes out right behind the wood panels in the Ambassador's private office. Admiral Aiken supervised the whole installation. They had to break through the cellar walls at night, and work in absolute silence."

"Is that why Lord Harlow sell other properties?" Israel asked excitedly. "Not to pay gambling debts. Need money to buy Binney Street house, do all construction."

"And paying workmen to keep quiet," Silas added. "Plus the cost of all that brass tubing. Must have been a fortune."

Silas glanced around to ensure Luke was still occupied elsewhere. "And one more thing. We found letters between Lord Harlow and Professor Varga about something called 'The Budapest Circle.' Seems there was whole network of aristocrats across Europe working to monitor Russian expansion. His lordship wasn't just gathering intelligence for England. He was part of something much larger."

Israel sat back, absorbing it all. The manor house in Gloucestershire, the gambling debts, the meetings - every piece was fitting together into a picture far more complex than any of them had imagined.

"You will tell Reed this?" Silas asked. "Before he meets Litvinov tonight?"

Israel nodded. "Yes, he must know everything." He hesitated, then added quietly, "Reed is... very special to me now."

Silas's expression softened. "I thought as much. The way he looks at you..." He smiled. "It's the same way Ezra looks at me."

Israel felt his face grow warm, but before he could respond, the door opened and Richard Pemberton swept in, bringing with him the smell of tobacco and morning fog.

"Ah, our mathematical genius returns," he said cheerfully. "I trust we'll have you back with us once this business with Russians is concluded?"

"If you still want me," Israel said.

"My dear fellow, anyone who can unravel conspiracy through account books is exactly the sort of person we need." Pemberton hung up his coat. "Though perhaps we can find you more legitimate mysteries to solve in future."

As Israel left the office later that morning, his heart was light despite the dangerous evening ahead. He had work he enjoyed, friends who accepted him, and Reed... Reed was something else entirely, something precious he was only beginning to understand.

He hurried toward Bloomsbury Square, eager to share what Silas had discovered. The knowledge about the listening posts under the Russian Embassy might prove crucial in their confrontation with Litvinov. And tomorrow, God willing, they could begin to build whatever future awaited them.

Chapter 33
Tea with a Lord
Reed

After Israel left Bloomsbury Square on Friday morning, a boy came to the door with an urgent message for Reed from Lord Ashworth. It was a summons for him and Cadence to meet that afternoon for tea at the Travellers' Club on Pall Mall, that bastion of men who had voyaged at least five hundred miles from London.

Because of Lord Ashworth's position in the government, even Cadence's period of mourning would not prevent them from attending. After sending their response back with the boy, Reed and Cadence went to the salon together so that Reed could show Cadence what he had learned about the condition of Drayton House.

The morning light filtered through the tall windows of the salon, casting gentle shadows across the William Morris wallpaper. Reed sat in his favorite chair with a volume of Keats, though his eyes kept straying to Cadence as she read through the papers they had brought from Drayton House. Her blonde curls were hidden beneath a widow's cap, and her black bombazine dress seemed to absorb what little cheerfulness remained in the room.

She looked up suddenly. "Thompson kept such detailed records of these meetings. Three men, always the same three. Lord Ashworth, Commodore Aiken, and this Professor Varga." She shuffled through the papers. "But what were they doing there? Why meet at our country house rather than here in London?"

"Privacy, I expect," Reed said. "London has too many eyes, too many chances of being observed. And Drayton House is perfectly situated. It's close enough to reach by train, remote enough to avoid unwanted attention."

"And Denis sold off those properties to fund this intelligence work?" Her voice caught slightly. "All this time I thought he was gambling away our fortune, and instead he was..." She trailed off, dabbing at her eyes with a black-bordered handkerchief.

"He was serving his country," Reed finished gently. "Though I suspect Lord Ashworth will be able to tell us more about that."

"The house is in such a state," Cadence said. "Thompson showed you the water damage? And the north wing roof?"

"Israel worked out a schedule for repairs," Reed said, unable to keep a note of pride from his voice. "If we can maintain current income from the estate, everything can be put right within eighteen months."

Cadence gave him a knowing look. "Israel seems to have worked out rather a lot of things." When Reed felt his face grow warm, she added, "Oh, don't look so uncomfortable, dear brother. After all, you've been very understanding about Mr. Wigton's visits."

"That's different," Reed protested. "Wigton is... well, he's..."

"Exactly what I need," Cadence finished. "Just as Israel appears to be exactly what you need." She set down the papers and came to perch on the arm of his chair, something she hadn't done since they were children. "We've both been so lonely, Reed. Perhaps it's time we allowed ourselves some happiness."

"You're still in mourning," he reminded her.

"Yes, and I shall observe all the proper forms. Antony has taught me well."

Reed noted the use of Wigton's first name, a familiarity he hadn't expected from Cadence. They heard the bell, and a moment later Joe

The Lord's Gambit

appeared at the door of the salon. "Mr. Israel," he said, and stepped back to allow Israel to enter the room.

"I did not expect to see you until this evening," Reed said. "At the Langham. Has something changed?"

"I will be there," Israel said. "But I must tell you what Silas discover."

He sat on a wing chair across from the desk and relayed what he had learned that morning about the house on Binney Street, and the depth of the work that Denis had been doing.

"Amazing," Reed said. "We shall have to relay all this information to Gervase Quinn."

"Silas already preparing documents for you to deliver after you meet with Litvinov," Israel said. "You say Quinn will be there?"

"In the background, yes. Why don't you bring them with you—in case something happens and I am unable to deliver them."

Cadence looked at him in alarm. "What do you mean?"

Reed shrugged. "Litvinov is a dangerous man. It is best that we don't keep all our cards in one hand."

He leaned over and squeezed her hand. "You should prepare for the Travellers' Club. Lord Ashworth won't appreciate tardiness."

As he watched her go up to change into her outdoor things, Reed marveled at how their lives had altered in just a few days. From the despair of bankruptcy to the hope of something better for both of them. Though first they had to get through this meeting, and then the confrontation with Litvinov that evening.

Israel left for Pemberton's office. When Cadence returned, correctly attired in her widow's weeds and veil, Reed offered her his arm. Together they stepped out into the March afternoon, ready to learn the final truth about Denis's secret life.

The carriage took Reed and Cadence through the early afternoon fog. Reed paused at the bottom of the steps leading to the Travellers' Club, drawing Cadence to a halt beside him. The fog was lifting, and the Portland stone of the building's facade took on a soft, ethereal quality.

"Look up there," Reed said quietly to his sister, pointing to where carved acanthus leaves adorned the capitals of the columns. "The same design appears in the Houses of Parliament. Both buildings were designed by Charles Barry, though this one came first."

He felt Cadence's hand trembling slightly in his and squeezed it. This was her first venture into society since Denis's death, and though the private nature of their meeting with Lord Ashworth meant she wasn't technically breaking mourning protocol, he knew how difficult it was for her.

The club's imposing entrance, with its great paneled door and brass fittings polished to a soft gleam, seemed to represent all the social barriers she would face in the coming months. People might never know what Denis had sacrificed, and regard her as the widow of a suicide, a dissolute gambler.

But as they mounted the stone steps, Reed noticed her spine straightening, her chin lifting. The rusticated stonework of the ground floor gave way to elegant first-floor windows with their triangular pediments. It was a subtle reminder that appearances could be deceptive, that grandeur often concealed secrets.

Just like Denis himself, Reed thought, as he handed his card to the porter. His rakish brother-in-law had hidden his patriotism behind a carefully constructed facade, much as this building's severe exterior concealed the comfort and conspiracy of its interior rooms.

They were led to a private dining room paneled in dark wood, with heavy velvet curtains drawn against the afternoon light. A fire burned in the grate despite the spring weather, and Lord Ashworth stood warming his hands before it. He was older than Reed expected, with silver hair and the weathered face of a man who had spent time in harsh climates.

"Lady Harlow," he said, taking Cadence's hand. "I knew your husband well. Better than you might imagine."

"So I'm beginning to understand," Cadence said. Her voice was steady, but Reed saw how tightly she gripped her reticule.

Ashworth gestured them to chairs, then rang for tea. Only when the door was firmly closed did he speak again.

"Denis was a patriot," he said quietly. "Though he played the dissolute gambler to perfection. He chose to appear to fall into Litvinov's web while actually gathering evidence of his activities."

"But something went wrong," Reed said.

Ashworth nodded. "Litvinov began to suspect. He sent men to follow Denis, to watch the house. Then he made a terrible discovery. That Denis had a weakness that could be exploited."

"What weakness?" Cadence asked.

"You, my dear." Ashworth's voice was gentle. "Your beauty, your innocence, your reputation. Litvinov threatened to destroy you with scandal if Denis didn't hand over the evidence we'd gathered."

Reed felt Cadence stiffen beside him. "So he killed himself to protect me?"

"To protect you, and to protect the operation. We had agents placed throughout Eastern Europe, gathering intelligence about Russian expansion. If Litvinov had forced Denis to talk..." Ashworth shook his head. "The damage would have been catastrophic."

The door opened silently and a manservant entered with a teapot and three cups on a silver tray. Then he backed away and closed the door.

"Shall I pour?" Cadence asked, her voice taut.

"If you would, my dear," Ashworth said. "Cream and two sugars, please."

She poured his first and prepared it, then cups for herself and Reed, as she knew how they both took their tea.

It was only after he had sipped his tea that Reed said, "We have in our possession letters from Commodore Aitken to Denis describing the modifications to the house on Binney Street, and the network of informants Professor Vargas has assembled. Will it be safe to pass those on to Gervase Quinn?"

Ashworth nodded. "We did not want to involve his office officially in order to maintain the utmost secrecy. But once Litvinov's dealings are exposed, it is right that Quinn should know the whole story."

Cadence put her teacup down on the silver tray. "Did Denis leave any message for me?" she asked.

"He did." Ashworth withdrew an envelope from his coat. "He gave it to me the day before he died, with instructions to deliver it if things went wrong. I've been waiting for the right moment."

With trembling fingers, Cadence opened the envelope. Reed recognized Denis's bold handwriting:

"My dearest Cadence,

If you are reading this, then I have failed in my duty to protect both you and our nation. Know that every action I took was in service to England, and to you. I could not bear to see you destroyed by the scandal Litvinov threatened.

Forgive me for maintaining the pretense of the wastrel husband. It was necessary for my work, but it caused you pain I never intended. You deserved better than that.

The evidence we gathered is hidden where only Thompson can find it. When the time is right, it will come to light.

I'm sorry I couldn't be the husband you deserved. But I hope that in this final act, I can at least protect you from the consequences of my choices.

Yours always,

Denis"

Cadence pressed the letter to her chest, tears flowing freely now. "I never knew," she whispered. "All those nights I thought he was gambling away our fortune..."

"He was a more complicated man than any of us knew," Ashworth said. "And a braver one." He turned to Reed. "You have the evidence now?"

Reed nodded. "We're meeting Litvinov tonight."

"Be careful. He's cornered, and that makes him dangerous." Ashworth stopped to consider his words.

"Denis was more than just a patriot," he said quietly. "He was vital to our private intelligence network. Each of us played a specific role: my political connections in Parliament, Commodore Aiken's military intelligence through the Navy, and Professor Varga's continental connections. But we needed someone who could get close to Litvinov, someone the Russians would never suspect."

He sipped his tea. "It was Denis's idea to use Litvinov's own methods against him. He deliberately lost at cards to build up debts, substantial enough to gain Litvinov's trust. Through that connection, he was able to document how Litvinov was using gambling debts to influence votes in Parliament about Russian expansion toward India."

"Those debts don't actually exist, do they?" Reed asked. "I understand that Mr. Fitch took money owed to the house and returned it to your operation."

"That is true, though Litvinov was not aware of that. And there were still debts due to other gamblers, and Litvinov or one of his agents took those on. Under the law, Lady Harlow is not responsible for those."

"The house on Binney Street," Reed said. "The listening posts."

"Yes. Aiken designed the system, Varga provided intelligence about Russian diplomatic protocols, and Denis managed the operation. We were close to having enough evidence to expose Litvinov's entire network of compromised lords." Ashworth's face darkened. "But then something went wrong."

"What happened?" Cadence asked.

"Litvinov became suspicious. He discovered enough to know we were gathering evidence, but not the full extent of our operation. He threatened Denis, not just with scandal to you, my dear, but with exposing our entire network to his Russian masters."

"So Denis sacrificed himself to protect everyone," Reed said.

"If he'd lived, Litvinov could have forced him to reveal everyone involved. Not just us three, but our agents across Europe. Years of work, dozens of lives, all at risk." Ashworth's voice was gentle. "By taking his own life, he protected both you and the network."

"But now you're arresting Litvinov publicly," Cadence said. "Won't that expose everything?"

"No. He'll be arrested for blackmail, a simple case of a money-lender exploiting the aristocracy. The evidence you've gathered will be used only to prove his corruption, not to expose our intelligence operations. The Russians will lose their man in London, but they won't know how much we've learned about their plans for expansion."

"And the network continues," Reed said, understanding at last.

"It must. Russia's ambitions in Central Asia haven't changed. We've removed one threat, but there will be others."

Ashworth paused. "There's something else you should know. The night before his death, Lord Harlow told me he'd prepared detailed documents about the estate's inheritance, all clearly laying out that everything would pass to you, my dear. But when we went to retrieve them after his death, we found evidence that someone had been through his papers. Litvinov's men, we assume, searching for the evidence we'd gathered against them. They must have taken or destroyed the inheritance documents along with anything else they found."

Ashworth stood. He looked at Cadence. "Your husband died protecting something far larger than himself. I hope that brings you some comfort, as well as to know that his last thoughts were of you."

"It does, Lord Ashworth. Thank you."

As they prepared to leave, Ashworth touched Cadence's arm. "Your husband died a hero, Lady Harlow. Never doubt that."

Outside in the gathering dusk, Cadence took Reed's arm. "I feel as if I never really knew him," she said.

"Perhaps none of us did," Reed replied. "But at least now we can clear his name."

They walked home in silence, each lost in thoughts of the man they had misjudged, and the confrontation that lay ahead.

Chapter 34
Confrontation at the Langham
Reed

Reed entered the Palm Court at precisely 7:45, forcing himself to maintain an unhurried pace as he handed his hat and coat to the checkroom attendant. The soaring domed ceiling and intricate plasterwork spoke of grandeur and respectability, exactly the sort of place where Litvinov would feel safe meeting.

His naval training took over as he assessed the room. Three men reading newspapers were Quinn's agents, no doubt. A pair of American ladies taking tea. The elderly Earl of Marchmont asleep in a wing chair. A Hungarian violin player wandering among the tables.

He caught a glimpse of Israel, sitting alone at a table near the entrance, ostensibly studying a mathematics text. It had been Reed's suggestion to position him there, where he could observe anyone entering or leaving. Though his clothes had improved since their first meeting, Israel still had an academic air that made him nearly invisible in such a setting.

Reed chose a table that gave him a clear view of both entrances while keeping his back to a wall. A waiter appeared with the evening's menu printed on thick card stock. "Just coffee for now," Reed said. His mouth felt dry but he couldn't risk alcohol affecting his judgment.

The coffee arrived in delicate bone china, steam rising in the cool evening air. Reed checked his pocket watch. 7:55. In the foyer, he heard the steady tick of the magnificent Vulliamy clock that was the hotel's pride.

At precisely eight o'clock, Sergei Litvinov walked into the Palm Court.

Reed had expected someone more physically imposing. Litvinov was of medium height and build, clean-shaven, wearing a perfectly tailored suit. Only his eyes betrayed him. They were cold and calculating as they swept the room. He moved with the liquid grace of a predator, and Reed was suddenly very glad of Quinn's hidden men.

"Mr. Lydney." Litvinov's accent was barely noticeable. "How good of you to agree to meet."

"I had little choice," Reed said, gesturing to the empty chair. "Given your threats against my sister."

Litvinov sat, arranging his coat tails with fastidious care. "Ah yes, the lovely Countess. Such a shame about her husband. Gambling can be so destructive to a man's character." He smiled, showing even white teeth. "And his life."

Reed's hand clenched under the table, but he kept his voice steady. "We both know why Lord Harlow killed himself."

"Do we?" Litvinov signaled the waiter. "A glass of your best cognac, if you please. And for you, Mr. Lydney? No? Such a pity to drink alone."

The casual mention of drinking alone -- was it a reminder of Reed's naval days? A hint that Litvinov knew about his proclivities? Reed pushed the thought aside. "I have what you want," he said. "The railway documents, the evidence of your operation. All of it."

"Excellent." Litvinov sipped his cognac. "Then our business can be concluded quickly. You give me the documents, I withdraw my threats against your sister, and we need never meet again."

"And the other lords you're blackmailing? What about them?"

"I have no idea what you mean." Litvinov's voice hardened. "I am merely a businessman who occasionally lends money to those in need. Now, the documents?"

Reed reached for his briefcase, noting how Litvinov's body tensed slightly. Was he armed? In the corner of his eye, he saw one of Quinn's men fold his newspaper.

"Everything is here," Reed said, withdrawing a manila envelope. "All the documents Lord Harlow took, all the evidence of your activities."

Litvinov reached for the envelope, but Reed held it back. "First, you will sign this." He produced a letter he and Quinn had drafted, explicitly withdrawing all claims against Cadence and acknowledging that any statements about her conduct were false.

"Really, Mr. Lydney, is this necessary?"

"Sign it, or I walk out that door with everything Lord Harlow collected about your operation. I'm sure the Foreign Office would be very interested."

Litvinov's eyes narrowed, and for a moment Reed saw the steel beneath the sophisticated facade. Then he smiled again and produced a fountain pen from his waistcoat. "As you wish."

The moment Litvinov's signature was dry, Reed handed over the envelope. He watched as the Russian opened it and began to examine the contents.

Suddenly Litvinov's face contorted with rage. "These are forgeries!" He started to rise. "You dare to--"

"Those are copies," Reed said calmly. "The originals are already in the hands of the Foreign Office. Your signed confession will be delivered very quickly."

The transformation was instantaneous. Litvinov lunged across the table, his hand reaching inside his coat. But Quinn's men were faster. Before he could draw whatever weapon he carried, they had him by both arms.

"Sergei Litvinov," the senior agent said quietly, "you are under arrest for espionage and attempted blackmail of a peer of the realm."

As they led him away, Litvinov turned back to Reed. "This isn't over," he snarled in Russian. "You have no idea what forces you're dealing with."

Reed sat back, his hands shaking slightly as the tension drained away. Quinn approached, and Reed handed him the folder, and the document that Litvinov had signed.

"You did very well," Quinn said. "I had no idea the breadth of Litvinov's influence, or the subterranean group working against him."

"There's more," Reed said, and he motioned Israel to approach. "You may be interested to learn that there are listening tubes installed in the Russian Ambassador's office, which connects by wine vaults to the house on Binney Street."

Israel handed the folder he was holding to Quinn, who opened it and scanned the contents. "This is extraordinary," he said. "You found all this?"

"With the help of Mr. Kupersmit, and the offices of Barrister Pemberton."

"I should like to see you both in my office on Monday morning," he said. "After I have had a chance to review these documents and consider what happens next."

Reed looked at Israel, who nodded. "It would be our pleasure," Reed said.

Quinn shook hands with both men and then walked out.

"Is finished?" Israel asked softly.

Reed nodded. "For now, at least." He looked at Israel, managing a smile. "Fancy a proper dinner? I believe I owe you that much, at least."

"You owe me nothing," Israel said. "But dinner would be nice. Especially if we can discuss more poetry than politics."

Reed stood, steadier now. "I believe that can be arranged." Together they walked out of the Palm Court, leaving behind the final act of Denis's tragedy and moving toward whatever future awaited them.

Author's Note

Readers of the Ormond Yard historical romances will know that I enjoy bringing historical events into play in these stories.

Characters and plot here are a result of my own imagination, but "The Great Game" was real. According to a reference guide from Ohio State University, "The Great Game was a political and diplomatic confrontation that existed for most of the 19th century between the British Empire and the Russian Empire over Afghanistan and neighboring territories in Central and South Asia." Potential railway expansion played a large role in this strategy.

Though Lord Magnus Dawson, Toby Marsh, John Seales (Lord Therkenwell), Raoul Desjardins, the Honorable Sylvia Cooke, and Jessamine Cleaver do not appear in this book, the circle they have created continues to exist in my mind and I hope will feature in future books in the series.

Acknowledgments

Thanks again to my terrific editor, Randall Klein, and my talented cover designer, Kelly Nichols. Joanna Campbell Slan and Greg Lindeblom provided advice and moral support during the writing of this manuscript. The Nova University library housed the reference books I needed, and librarian extraordinaire Chris Caspar helped nudge me in the right directions.

As always, I appreciate the efforts of my beta readers: Tim Brehme, Andy Jackson, Bob Kman, and Faith Lapidus Weiner.

Any remaining errors, of course, are my fault.

If you are new to this series, you can find more information about the men of Ormond Yard and their romances at my website, www.mahubooks.com. I've also written many other books you might like, which you can find there as well.

www.ingramcontent.com/pod-product-compliance
Lightning Source LLC
LaVergne TN
LVHW012017060526
838201LV00061B/4344